Sanborn Tenney

Young Folks Pictures and Stories of Animals..

Sanborn Tenney

Young Folks Pictures and Stories of Animals..

ISBN/EAN: 9783744783835

Printed in Europe, USA, Canada, Australia, Japan

Cover: Foto ©Andreas Hilbeck / pixelio.de

More available books at **www.hansebooks.com**

YOUNG FOLKS'

PICTURES AND STORIES OF ANIMALS

FOR HOME AND SCHOOL

BY

MRS. SANBORN TENNEY

QUADRUPEDS

WITH EIGHTY-SEVEN WOOD ENGRAVINGS

BOSTON
LEE AND SHEPARD, PUBLISHERS
NEW YORK
CHARLES T. DILLINGHAM
1887

YOUNG FOLKS'
PICTURES AND STORIES OF ANIMALS
FOR HOME AND SCHOOL

By Mrs. Sanborn Tenney

In Six Volumes. Containing 500 Wood Engravings
Each Volume complete in itself

QUADRUPEDS

BIRDS

FISHES AND REPTILES

BEES, BUTTERFLIES, AND OTHER INSECTS

SEA SHELLS AND RIVER SHELLS

SEA-URCHINS, STAR-FISHES, AND CORALS

PREFACE.

———◆———

BELIEVING that there is nothing in which children are naturally more interested than they are in
animals, and that there are no other objects which
can be used to greater advantage than these in their
instruction, the writer has prepared these Pictures
and Stories of Animals for the Little Ones, to in-
struct as well as to interest and amuse them.

There are six books in the series, each one complete in itself; and they are so arranged that together they make a Juvenile Library of the Natural
History of Animals.

The first book contains pictures and stories of
Mammals or Quadrupeds; the second book, pictures
and stories of Birds; the third, of Reptiles and
Fishes; the fourth, of Bees, Butterflies, and other

Insects, and of Crustaceans and Worms; the fifth, of Shells, and the animals which live in them; and the sixth, of Sea-Cucumbers, Sea-Urchins, Star-Fishes, Jelly-Fishes, Sea-Anemones, and Corals.

The wood engravings in the six books are more than five hundred in number, and are true to nature. Several of them were drawn and engraved expressly for this series; the others are mainly from Tenney's "Manual of Zoölogy," "Natural History of Animals," and other works of Tenney's Natural History Series.

August, 1868.

CONTENTS.

PICTURES AND STORIES OF ANIMALS.

You have so much loved to look at the pictures of animals in the books upon your papa's table, that I think you will like to have some little books of your own, which have in them many pictures of animals and a little story about each one of them, telling you where it lives, how large it is, and what kind of a home it makes for itself and its little ones. You, Sanny, are too young to read, but I am sure you will love to have your sister read to you some of these little stories.

When you go to walk in the woods and fields, or to ride in the boat upon the pond, or when you are only looking out of the window, you often see several kinds of animals. Some kinds are large like the Horse and the Ox, and some are small like the

Squirrel which you saw the other day leaping so nimbly from bough to bough, or like the little shining Beetles which glide so swiftly over the water in the shady nook where we tie the boat. But you must not think that there are no animals larger than the Horse and the Ox, and none smaller than the Beetles; in this little book you will find a picture of the Elephant, an animal much larger than the largest ox; and of the Whale, the largest animal in the world; and there are animals so small that many hundreds of them can live in a single drop of water!

In this little book I shall show you pictures, and tell you stories of Mammals, or Quadrupeds, — the last word means Four-footed Animals.

Some kinds of animals have all their feet like hands, and such animals are made to live on trees, and they can climb well. As they seem to have four hands, they are called Four-handed Animals. On the next page there is a picture of one of them. Some of them, like the one in the picture, are often called Apes; others have a long tail, and are called Monkeys; and others have a long tail, and a head much like that of a dog, and

A Four-handed Animal.

are called Baboons. All of the Four-handed Animals live in warm countries, and I will soon tell
you more about them.

Some kinds of animals have very sharp teeth
and sharp claws, and they kill and eat other an-

A Flesh eater, or Beast of Prey.

imals, and they are called Flesh-eaters, or Beasts
of Prey.   Here is a picture of one of them.
Cats, Dogs, Wolves, Foxes, Hyenas, Weasels,
Bears, and Seals are Flesh-eaters.

Some kinds of animals are made to eat grass, leaves, and tender twigs of bushes and trees, and they are called the Plant-eaters. As their feet end in hoofs, they are often called the Hoofed Animals.

A Plant-eater, or Hoofed Animal.

Some kinds of animals are made to live in the sea, but are also made to breathe air, and so they have to come often to the surface of the water to get the air ; and they breathe through a hole on the top of their head. They are called Whales, and some of them are the largest animals in the world.

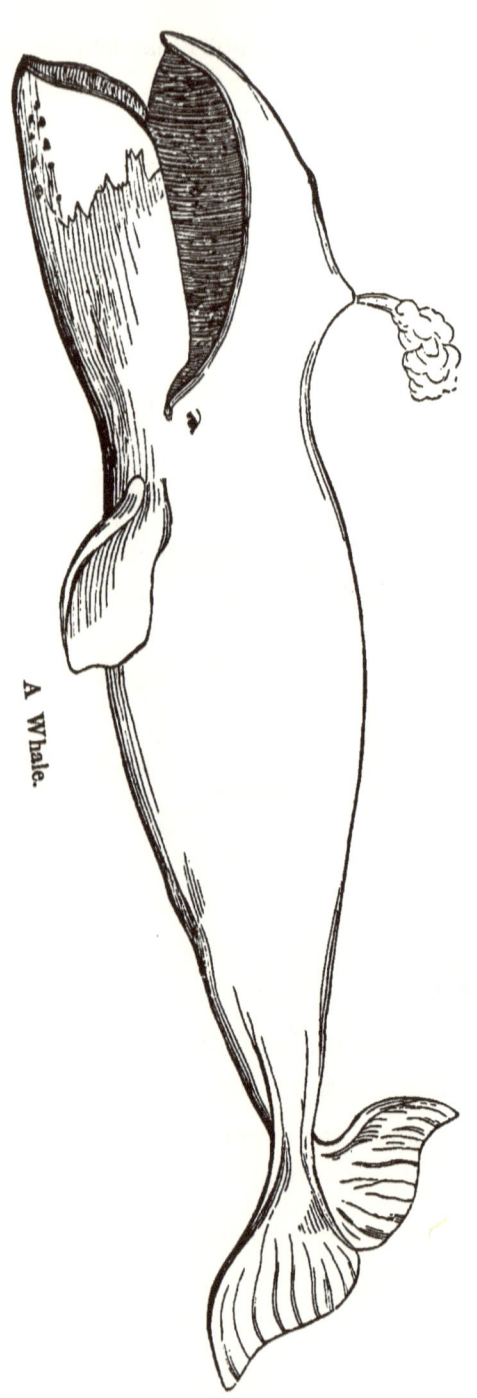

A Whale.

Some kinds of animals have broad thin wings, and are made to fly in the air like birds; they have no feathers, but are covered with fur, and the small ones look like a mouse with wings. They are called Bats.

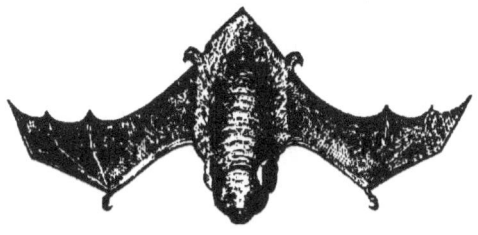

A Bat.

Some kinds of animals look like little mice, and are made to live in the ground, and to feed upon worms and little insects, and they are called Insect-eaters, and here is a picture of one of them.

An Insect-eater.

Some kinds of animals are made for feeding upon bark and nuts; they have strong sharp teeth, and can easily gnaw the bark from a tree, or gnaw into a nut and get the nice sweet food within. They are called the Gnawers. Beavers, Squirrels, Hares, Rats, and Mice are of this sort.

A Gnawing Animal.

Some kinds of animals have no front teeth; and others have no teeth at all. Some of these animals have fur, and others have a hard bony or horny covering. Here is a picture of one which has a hard

An Animal without front teeth.

horny covering. Of those animals which have
no teeth, the most curious are the Ant-eaters of
South America. They have a long tongue, covered with a sticky fluid, and they push their tongue
into the ant-nests, and the ants stick to it and
are drawn out and swallowed.

Some kinds of animals have a sack or pouch on
the under side of the body, in which they carry

A Pouched Animal.

their little ones before they are able to walk and run
about; and these are called the Pouched Animals.
The Opossum of our country and the Kangaroo
of Australia are of this kind.

And there are some kinds of animals that have a bill much like that of a duck, and webbed feet, and a body covered with fur; they are bird-like animals, and are called Duckbills. Here is a picture of one of these curious animals. It lives far away in Australia. No animals of this kind are found in our country.

A Bird-like Animal.

God has made some animals to live only in cold and frozen regions, where ice and snow cover the ground all of the year. He has made others to live in lands that are cold during one part of the year, and warm during the other part; and others, still, he has made, whose home is where it is always summer, where the trees are always green, and fruits grow in great abundance.

THE FOUR-HANDED ANIMALS.

It is in the warm countries that the Apes,
Monkeys, and Baboons live, — the curious animals,
whose feet look like hands.   There are many kinds
of these animals, and they are of all sizes, from
those no larger than a squirrel to those as large as
a man.   They live in the forests, mostly on the
trees ; for they are fitted for climbing, and for leaping from tree to tree and from limb to limb.   Some
kinds of monkeys have a long tail which they can
twist around the branches, and thus use it as a
hand in climbing.   All of these animals eat fruits
and nuts, and also birds' eggs and insects.   Some
kinds have a pouch or sack on each side of the
mouth, in which they can carry food.   Many of
them are playful, and all are selfish and thievish,
and full of mischief.

The Gorilla is the largest of the Apes.   It lives
in Africa, and it is larger than a man, and so
powerful that it can tear a man to pieces in a
moment.

Another very large ape is the Chimpanzee, which

The Chimpanzee.

lives in Guinea, in Africa, and looks so much like
a man, that, in his own country, he is called by

The Orang-Outang.

a name which means "man of the forest." The
Chimpanzees live together in large numbers, and

The Kahau.

The Marmoset.

The Spider-Monkey.

The Lemur.

build a sort of nest or hut among the branches of large trees. Another large ape is the Orang-Outang whose picture I have shown you on another page. This ape lives on the island of Borneo.

The Orang, like the Chimpanzee, builds nests of leaves and branches.

The Kahaus, or Long-nosed Monkeys, live together in large numbers in Borneo and the southern part of India, and as they bound and frolic they cry *kahau, kahau.* They are about the size of a large dog.

There are many kinds of monkeys in South America, and most of them have a long tail, and the tail is so made that they can pick up things with it as if it were a hand, and they can grasp with it the branches of trees, and thus use it in climbing; and some kinds can put their tail so firmly around the limbs of the trees that they can let go with their hands and swing by the tail, without falling. Some kinds of the South American monkeys make loud and frightful yells in the night; these are called the Howlers. Some kinds have long, sprawling, spider-like legs, and are called Spider-Monkeys. Some kinds make a mournful cry, and so they are called the Weepers. Some kinds have a long bushy tail like that of a fox, and so they are called the Fox-tailed Monkeys. Some kinds look so much like squirrels that they are called Squirrel-Monkeys. The little Marmosets also look like squirrels as they nimbly run about and leap from tree to tree; their fur is long, soft, and beautiful, and they are so gentle and graceful that some people keep them for pets.

The Lemurs are monkey-like little animals which live on the island of Madagascar. They are very pretty, with soft silky fur, and a large bushy tail. In the same island lives the Aye-Aye, a curious, monkey-like animal, about the size of a cat, with

The Aye-Aye.

large ears, and with teeth much like those of a squirrel. It digs a hole in the ground, in which it sleeps in the daytime, coming out at night for its food.

THE FLESH-EATERS, OR BEASTS OF PREY.

You like the cat, and love to have her lie in your lap, where you can feel her soft fur, and listen to her purring, as you gently stroke her with your hand. She is very tame and does not scratch nor bite. But the house cats were once wild, and lived in the woods, though they have long been tame as you see them now. There are, however, many kinds of cats which are wild and live in the forests, and are never handled except by daring men, who sometimes get them when they are young, and train them so that they can handle them and play with them as you do with your pretty kittens. These cats are called Lions, Tigers, Leopards, Panthers, Pumas, and Lynxes. You have never heard these animals called cats before, but they are true cats, and they have sharp teeth, and sharp claws, and cushions on the bottoms of their feet, so that they can step softly, and they watch for their prey, and when they have stealthily crept near to it, they pounce upon it with a spring, just as you have seen your puss spring upon a mouse or a bird. These great fierce cats eat sheep, deer, antelopes, and other large animals, and when they get a chance, even man himself.

The Lion.

The Lion is one of the largest of the cats, and

lives in Africa, and in the southern part of Asia.
He is as long as an ox, but does not stand so
high; the color is pale dingy yellow, and the long
tail ends in a tuft of black hair, and the head
and neck are clothed with a long, full, flowing
mane. His head is very large; and, when the
Lion is angry, his eyes flame like fire, his mane
stands erect, he shows his teeth, and thrusts out
his claws which are as long as a man's fingers,
and he is then very terrible to look upon. The
strength of the Lion is very great; one stroke
of his paw will crush the head of the great buffalo,
and he can carry off the body of a man as easily
as a cat can carry off a mouse.

The Lion is often called the "king of the forest," but he does not live so much in the forest
as on the plains, and in those places where the
antelopes go to feed. Like the house cat, the
Lion almost always spends the day in rest and
sleep, and hunts his prey at night; and he hides
and lies in wait, or creeps slowly towards his
victim, and then springs forward upon it with
a bound, and sometimes with a dreadful roar.
The roar of the Lion is very terrific; the Arabs

call it by a word which means thunder. It is
said that Lions are more active and furious on
those nights when storms are raging, and their
roarings, together with the thunder, the torrents
of rain, and the vivid flashes of lightning, make
the night one of horror to the traveller encamped
upon the plains or in the forest. When the ani.
mals which are resting on the plains hear the
roar of the Lion, they start up frightened, and
bound away, and, in their terror, often rush towards the spot where the Lion is crouching ready
to spring upon them.

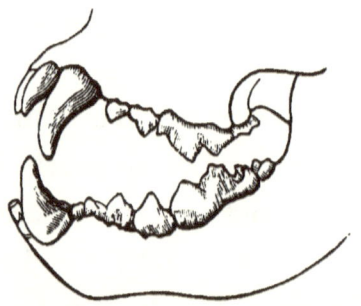

The Teeth of a Flesh-eater.

I have told you that all the cats have very
sharp teeth; they are made to eat the flesh of
other animals, and their back teeth do not shut
upon each other to crush food as yours do, but

the teeth in the upper and lower jaws shut by each other like the blades of a pair of scissors, and thus they cut the flesh in pieces. The tongue of the cat is very curious; you know how rough your little kitten's tongue is; the Lion's tongue is much more rough, so rough that if he should lick a man's hand, as kitty sometimes licks yours, he would tear away the skin.

The Lion and Lioness take good care of their young ones; they guard them from harm, and bring them tender food to eat, and when they are about five or six months old, they take them out to hunt, and to teach them to kill for themselves. The young Lions stay with their parents about three years; when they are eight years old they are full-grown, and they live thirty or forty years.

Many daring men like to hunt these fierce, savage animals, and the hunters and the travellers, who have visited the countries in which Lions live, have told us much about them. We are told that the Lion often lies in wait near springs of water, so as to attack the animals that come to drink, and it is said that when the Lion springs upon a giraffe, — a tall, beautiful animal that I shall tell you about by and by, — he is sometimes carried for miles fixed to the neck of the fleet creature, before it sinks bleeding and dying under him.

The negroes know that the Lion is found on the open plains, and near the herds of antelopes, and that he kills and eats his prey at evening and very early in the morning; and so when they wish to kill Lions, they watch the herds feeding on the plains, and if they seem frightened and run, they know that they have been attacked by Lions, so they mark the spot, and at noon when the sun is hot, they cautiously come near, and almost always find the Lion sleeping, and then they shoot him with a poisoned arrow. The Lions often come near towns and settlements to attack the cattle, and sometimes the people. A story is told of a man who was driving some cattle to drink, and who saw that he was pursued by a Lion; the man ran to a tree, up which he climbed; the Lion followed and lay down at the foot of the tree; all day and all night the Lion waited, and the man remained in the tree; at last the Lion became so thirsty for water, that he went away to drink, and while he was gone the man fled to his home, which was about a mile away; the Lion returned to the tree, and, finding the man gone, he followed him nearly to his door.

The Royal Tiger is as large as the lion, but it has a smaller head. It lives in the southern part of Asia, and on the large islands of that region. Though not so noble looking as the lion, it is a more graceful animal, and its colors are much more beautiful. It is yellow, handsomely striped with black, and underneath it is almost pure white. When pleased it purrs, and rubs itself against any object which is near, just as you have often seen your kitty rub herself against the sofa or the legs of the table. The Tiger is said to be more fierce than the lion. It lurks in the jungles and forests, and among the bushes that grow along the river-banks, and springs upon its prey, sometimes leaping as many as fifty feet to secure it. It is often easily frightened. A lady in India, seeing a Tiger about to spring upon some people, frightened it away by quickly opening an umbrella before it!

Horses have such a dread of Tigers that they are not much used in hunting these fierce animals. So the tiger-hunters ride to the hunt upon elephants, which are not so easily frightened, and stand more steadily, and are so powerful that when the Tiger springs upon them, they are almost always able to shake him off.

The Tiger is very strong, and very swift in its motions. Once, during the march of an army through a forest, a Tiger sprang upon a horseman, snatched him from the saddle, and bore him off into the woods before any one could give help to the poor man.

The Jaguar, or American Tiger, is a very powerful and very fierce cat which lives in Texas, Mexico, and South America. It is smaller than the Royal Tiger of India, and it is of a yellowish color, marked and spotted with black. It preys upon all kinds of animals which it can catch, and it often lies in wait near springs and streams, where animals come to drink, and from behind a bush, or from the branches of a tree, it leaps down upon young cattle, deer, and horses, and fastens its sharp teeth in some poor animal's neck,

while its sharp claws are struck deep into his
back and sides. The poor creature is soon killed,
and then the Jaguar begins to eat it. The Jaguar
never runs after its prey as wolves do, but follows it slyly and stealthily. It will sometimes
follow a man for a long time, that it may get a
chance to spring upon him suddenly. The Jaguars
swim across rivers, and they sometimes plunge into
the water and attack the Indian in his canoe.

The Leopard lives in Africa and in Asia. It
is about half as large as the Tiger; its form is
elegant, and its movements are very graceful. Its
skin is very beautiful; the color is pale yellow,
covered all over the back and sides with roundish
spots of black, but fading into white below. The
Leopard is very active, and he swims, bounds,
creeps, and climbs trees. He is often called the
Tree-Tiger, because he runs up the trees so easily,
and leaps about from branch to branch; sometimes he crouches and stretches himself along a
limb, so that he can scarcely be noticed, and lies
there waiting to spring down upon some animal
which is passing beneath. Leopards eat small
antelopes, deer, and little monkeys. Those that

live near settlements come and steal sheep and pigs, and they will attack man if they can creep up behind him. The Leopard is easily tamed, and plays like a kitten. The Panther looks very much like the Leopard, and it is found in the same countries.

The Puma is a cat which lives in the forests of our country, and it is as large as the largest dog. It is sometimes called the American Lion; it is also called the Panther, and the Catamount, or Cat of the Mountain. It is long and slender, and its color is a silvery-fawn, or reddish gray, upon the back, and it is nearly white below. It eats young deer, raccoons, hares, birds, and other small animals; it often climbs trees, and lies upon a limb, ready to spring upon its prey as it passes under the tree; and it sometimes comes to the farm-yards and kills the sheep and lambs. Unless very hungry, it will not attack man in the daytime, but it will sometimes spring upon him at night, — for, like other cats, it prowls about at night for its food. But it is afraid of fire, and so the woodsman and the traveller frighten away the Puma by keeping up a blazing fire all night.

In the mountains the Puma's den is near the mouth of some cave in the rocks, and only just far enough in to be sheltered from the rain; in the marshy lands the Puma's lair is in a dense

The Puma.

thicket, or among the tall weeds and grass. The Puma sometimes utters a wild, startling cry or growl, which is not pleasant to hear. The Puma is very bloodthirsty, and it has been known to kill fifty sheep in one night, for the sake of sipping a little blood from each one of them.

The Canada Lynx lives in the forests of the northern parts of our country, and is as large as a good-sized dog, and its ears are tipped with long black hairs. Its feet are very large, and its claws are long and sharp. The Lynx catches hares,

The Canada Lynx.

squirrels, and partridges, pursuing the birds even among the tree-tops. The Wild-Cat is very much like the Lynx, but is smaller, and has no long hairs on the tips of its ears. It lives in the woods in nearly all parts of our country, and it sometimes comes to the farm-yard to get the hens and chickens.

You, dear Sanny, are so fond of watching a dog, that I know you will like to look at this picture of a

Wolf, — an animal which looks very much like a large dog, but which lives in the woods, and in the wild, unsettled parts of our country. Wolves are very strong, fierce, greedy animals, and often hunt in large companies or packs, and thus they

The Wolf.

can kill animals which are much larger than themselves, and which one Wolf alone would not dare to attack. They chase and overtake the reindeer, and kill and eat it. They prowl about the herds of buffaloes, and snatch up the young which stray too far from the herd, or any that are left behind when the herd moves on. In the newly settled parts of the country they catch sheep, lambs, and young cattle, and thus do great injury to the farmer. They sometimes catch and eat dogs and foxes. They can overtake a fox in running, and a single wolf is so powerful that he can carry off a fox or a dog in his mouth. I have heard a true story of a wolf that came prowling around a fort where there were soldiers; and one day he was shot at, and hit with a bullet and driven away; at night he came back to the fort, and although still bleeding from his wound, he stole one of the fifty dogs which were kept there, and carried it off in his mouth. The wolves in this country do not often attack men; but in Russia, and in some other countries of Europe, they are more fierce, and they often attack travellers who are passing through forests or lonely places.

The Dog is found in every country. He likes to be near man, and is his faithful servant and friend; and he is the only animal that has gone with man to all parts of the world. There are many different sorts of dogs. Some are very small, so small that you could hold one of them in your hands; and others are so large and strong that one of them could easily carry you on his back, or draw you if he were harnessed to a cart. Some

The Shepherd's Dog.
The Setter.
The Bloodhound.
The Bull-dog
The Pointer.
The Terrier.
The King Charles Spaniel.

The Greyhound.
The Fox.
The Saint Bernard.

The Newfoundland Dog.

The Esquimaux Dog.
The Foxhound.
The Poodle.
The Coach Dog.
The Mastiff.

kinds of dogs are pretty for pets; others are pleasant companions; others are good for hunting birds,
squirrels, and other small game; others for hunting large wild beasts; others for guarding houses
and stores; others for tending sheep, or driving
cattle; others for drawing loads; and one or two
noble kinds of dogs are good for helping those that
are in trouble and danger. You will like to know
the names of some of these different kinds, and
you will like to read some true stories about them.

One very beautiful kind has a long slender body,
covered with smooth, shining hair; a small, pointed
head; a long, curved tail; and long, slender legs.
This is the Greyhound. It is the swiftest of all
the dogs, and it is used in hunting deer, foxes, and
hares, and other swift-running animals, and it follows them by sight, and not by smelling their
tracks as other hunting dogs do.

The Saint Bernard Dog is very large and strong,
with a large head, long hair, and a bushy tail.
This noble dog is so kind, so intelligent, and so useful, that I must tell you all about him. He is sometimes called the Alpine Spaniel, because his home
is among the Alps, — high mountains in Switzer-

land, a country beyond the sea. There are several
roads or passes which lead over these mountains
to Italy, and in some places the roads are very steep
and narrow, and in the winter season they are very
dangerous. There are snow-storms on these mountains, even in the summer months, but in the long
winter season they are very violent. These storms
sometimes come on very suddenly, often when the
morning has been bright and pleasant; and they
rage with so much fury, and the snow falls to such
depths, that, in a few hours, the traveller is buried
beneath the drifts. Many persons have lost their
lives in trying to pass over these mountains during the winter season.

One of the most dangerous of the passes over
these mountains is that of the Grand St. Bernard.
In some places, on one side of the pass you can
look down over the rocks several hundred feet,
while on the other side are high cliffs, and the
path itself is often slippery with snow and ice.
Great masses of rock, ice, and snow overhang the
path, and sometimes these are loosened by the
storms and winds that sweep over these regions,
and they fall upon the path, and over the precipice,

and carry away or bury the poor traveller, or fill the path so that he cannot make his way, and he sinks down, weary and cold, and soon falls asleep, while the snows blow and drift over him.

The pass of the Grand Saint Bernard was used before Christ lived upon the earth ; and, for nearly a thousand years there has been, near the top of the mountain, and not far from the pass, a stone house, in which travellers may find food and shelter. This house was founded by a good monk named Bernard de Menthon. At first the house was very small, but now it is a large building, four stories high, and can contain many people. It is called the Convent, or Hospice of Saint Bernard. Here good monks live all the year, for the purpose of aiding travellers. And here are kept the noble Saint Bernard dogs, and, with the help of these dogs, the monks are able to save many lives. From ten to twenty thousand persons go over this pass every year, and all are made welcome to the Hospice. In this cold, dreary region nothing will grow, and all the food, and the wood with which it is cooked, must be carried up the mountain during the short summer of three months.

But I must tell you about the good dogs. They are trained to look for lost travellers, and every day in winter they are sent out, almost always in pairs; one has a basket of food and a flask of wine or brandy strapped to his neck, the other has a cloak strapped upon his back, so that if they find some poor fainting man, he may be supplied with food and clothing. If the man can walk, they lead him towards the convent, barking loudly for help, and to let the monks know that they are coming back. If the man cannot move, they go back, and guide the monks to the spot where he is. Sometimes the traveller is covered by ten, or even twenty feet of snow, and if the monks were alone they could not find him; but the keen scent of the dogs discovers him, and they scratch up the snow with their feet, and they bark until the monks come to the spot. But the dogs themselves sometimes perish in their attempts to save the lives of others. One cold stormy night, more than fifty years ago, a man was crossing the mountains, on his way to his home in a little village in the valley on the other side. After great trouble and danger he got to the Hospice, and the monks tried to have him stay there all the night, and finish his journey the next day. But he was very anxious about his little family, and would not stay; so they gave him two guides, and two dogs to go with him, and they all started down the mountain together. The same night his wife and children became so alarmed at his long absence that they left their home and began to go up the mountain, hoping to meet him, or to hear from him. While they were toiling up, and he was coming down, great masses of ice and snow were loosened from the top of the mountain, and they swept down into the valley below, and all these good people, and the faithful dogs were covered up and destroyed. One of these dogs had saved the lives of twenty-two persons. Another dog, named Barry, saved during his lifetime the lives of forty-two persons, all of whom must have perished if it had not been for him. When he died, his skin was stuffed, and placed in the museum at Berne. I will tell you a story which is told of Barry. A mother, who was going up the mountain with her little son, was carried away by a snow-slide. Barry found the little boy unhurt, but cold and stiff; in some way he induced him to get upon his back, and thus carried him to the door of the Hospice, where he was taken good care of by the monks.

The Newfoundland Dog is very large, and is covered with long shaggy hair, which is black or very dark in color. He is good-natured, obedient, and faithful. He loves his master and his master's family, and he seems to understand their wishes, and he carefully guards their home. He is a pleasant companion at home, and in the fields, and on the river when you go a-boating. He is very kind to children, and if he sees a child fall into the river, this noble dog quickly plunges in and saves the little one from drowning, and he has often saved men from being drowned. A little girl was on board of a ship with her mamma, and on the same ship was a gentleman who had with him a fine Newfoundland Dog. The little girl wished to play with the dog, but her mamma, fearful that the great dog would hurt her, would not allow it. By and by the little girl fell into the sea, and a great cry was raised for the life-boat. All the time the ship was moving on, and the little girl was left behind struggling in the water. But before the boat was made ready, the noble dog had leaped into the water; he swam to the drowning girl, seized her dress, and swam to the boat which had been launched, and both were soon safe in the ship.

Once, when a dreadful storm was raging, a vessel was driven upon the coast of England. The waves were running very high, so that no boat could be launched, and yet eight poor men on board the vessel were calling for help. At last a gentleman came upon the beach, and with him was a Newfoundland Dog. The man pointed to the vessel, and put a short stick in the dog's mouth. The brave fellow knew his meaning, and sprang into the water, and swam through the waves towards the vessel; he could not get near enough to the vessel to give the stick, but the men knew what was meant, and they fastened a rope to another piece of wood, and threw it towards the dog, and the noble creature dropped his own piece, seized the one that had been thrown to him, and swam towards the shore, and though several times lost under the waves, he reached the land, and gave the stick with the rope tied to it to his master, and thus those on shore could help those on the vessel, and they were saved.

In Newfoundland these dogs are trained to draw carts and sledges.

The Esquimaux Dog lives with the Esquimaux, half-savage people of Greenland, and other cold regions of the North. This dog has short, pointed ears, which stand erect, a bushy tail, which curves over the back, and stout legs. It has a thick coat of hair, which in winter is very long. It also has, in winter, an under coating of close, soft wool. This dog never barks, but it utters a long, wild howl, like that of the wolf. It is almost as savage as a wolf, and it has no love for its master, and obeys him only through fear. But the Esquimaux Dogs are very useful; for their masters harness them to a sort of sled, called a sledge, and the dogs thus draw their masters and heavy loads over the snow with great speed. From six to twelve dogs are harnessed to each sled, and they are guided by means of a long whip; the driver uses no reins.

The Shepherd's Dog is large, of a black or dark

color, and it has a slender pointed nose, short
ears, long shaggy hair, and a bushy tail. A shepherd is a man who takes care of sheep, and the
Shepherd's Dog helps him do this work. He helps
his master guard the flock from the attacks of
wolves and other wild beasts, and he helps him
gather the flock into the fold at night; and when
the day's work is done, he goes home with his
master, sits by his side while he is eating his
supper, or curls up close to his chair and falls
asleep. When the flocks are very large, and have
to be guarded at night, or when cold storms come
on, and the sheep and lambs must be gathered
into some safe warm place, then the Shepherd's
Dog is of great service; for he must run over the
hills, often for miles; he does this quickly and
gets his master's flock all together, and does not
get them mixed with the sheep of other flocks.
One dark night in Scotland, many years ago, a
large flock of lambs which a shepherd was guarding
became greatly frightened, and ran away in different directions across the hills. The shepherd
told his dog that they were all gone; and the
shepherd spent the whole night in looking for the

lambs, but could not find them. The dog, too, was missing. The shepherd was feeling very badly, thinking that he would have to go home and tell the master that the lambs were lost. But, on his way home, to his great joy he found the lambs gathered in a deep ravine, and faithfully guarded by his dog; not a lamb was missing. The noble fellow had collected the scattered lambs in the dark, and gathered all together, and was guarding them till the shepherd should come.

A shepherd once went out upon the hills to look after his flock, and he took with him his little child who was about four years old. By and by the shepherd found that he must go up a high hill, which was so steep that the little child could not go with him, so he left him at the bottom of the hill, and told him not to move from the place. Soon after the shepherd got to the top of the hill, a thick mist came on, so that the day was almost like night. The shepherd went back to look for his child, but could not find him, and after searching a long time, he had to go back to his cottage without him. His dog, also, was not to be found. Early the next morn-

ing, the shepherd again began to search for his
dear child, but again he had to go back without
him. But when he got home he learned that his
dog had returned, and as soon as he received his
food had gone again. For four days the shepherd
looked for his child, without finding any trace
of him, and every day the dog came for food
and went away again. At last the man thought
he would follow the dog, and the dog led him to
a steep place among the rocks, at some distance
from the spot where the child had been left; the
dog went down the rocks and entered a sort of
cave at the bottom; the shepherd followed, and
there he found his little child eating the bread
which the dog had brought to him. The child
had wandered away from the spot where he was
left, and had fallen or scrambled down the rocks;
the dog had tracked him, and when he found
him, never left him day nor night, except when
he went for food.

The Fox-Hound is a large dog, with long drooping ears; it is used in hunting foxes. It runs
faster than the fleetest horses, and is very highly
prized by the hunters. In England a gentleman

sometimes keeps fifty or sixty Fox-Hounds to aid him and his friends in fox-hunting. These gentlemen do not shoot the fox, but they chase it with dogs and horses till the poor animal is overtaken and killed by the dogs. The kennels which are built for the hounds are often large and costly. The dog-kennel of the Duke of Richmond cost thirty thousand dollars.

The Bloodhound is a very large, stout, and very fierce dog, which has often been used in hunting men who had escaped from those who wished to capture them.

The Spaniels are dogs which came from Spain, and so they are called Spaniels. There are very many kinds of them. They have large drooping ears, and long silky fur. They have a bright, pleasant look, and they are kind and affectionate. One is the King Charles Spaniel, a pretty little pet dog. Another is called the Setter, and this is a favorite with hunters, for it aids them in hunting quail, grouse, and woodcock. I will tell you a true story about a little Spaniel. One morning as its mistress was lacing her boots, one of the laces broke, and she turned to the dog and said playfully, " O dear! I wish you would find me another boot-lace." Then she tied the broken one, and thought no more about it. On the next morning, when she was again lacing her boots, her little Spaniel ran up to her with a new silken boot-lace in his mouth, but where he got it no one could tell.

The Pointer is a large dog, which looks both like a hound and a setter, and is also used in hunting quail, grouse, and woodcock. When he comes near the game, he stops, lifts one foot, looks steadily at the game, and points towards it with his nose, and he does not move till the hunter tells him to go forward and " flush," or start up the bird. The dog then moves forward, and when the bird flies, the hunter takes good aim and shoots it; then the dog, if well trained, will go and get the bird and bring it to his master. If the hunter does not bid him go and bring the bird, the dog stands still until his master tells him what to do. Some Pointers are so well trained that they will stand perfectly motionless for an hour, or even longer. Two dogs of this kind were made to point while an artist could make a sketch of them. This took him an hour and a quarter, and the dogs stood perfectly still all that time.

The Poodle is small, with broad, hanging ears, and with long, thick, curly hair, and is a nice dog for a pet. You have often seen this little dog.

The Terriers are also good pet dogs, for they are good-natured, and fond of play and frolic. One of these dogs used to play at hide-and-seek with his master. When his master said, " Come, let us have a game," the dog would cover his eyes with his paws; then his master would hide a cake, or a piece of money, and the dog would get up and look till he found it. The Terriers seem to understand what is told them, and they learn very easily to perform curious feats. They are full of courage, and do not hesitate to attack the fox or the wolf. They get the name of Terrier from the word *terra*, which means earth; because, these dogs, being small, and fierce in hunting, are sometimes sent into holes in the earth to drive out the game, as foxes and rabbits. They are good for catching and killing rats.

The Mastiff is a large, strong, but very good-natured dog; he is much attached to his master, and always ready to defend him, and everything which belongs to him. He is kept as a watch-dog, and it is often dangerous for a stranger to try to enter the house, or stable, against his will.

The Bull-dog is fierce and ugly looking. He has a thick round head, thick lips, and a turned-up nose. He has great strength and courage.

Foxes are smaller than wolves and most of the dogs, and they have a slender nose, and a large bushy tail. They do not go in droves, but hunt alone, and they hunt only at night, and in the early morning. They dig holes in the ground, where they rear their young, and where they often stay in the daytime. Sometimes they spend the day in dense thickets, or under a fallen tree-top, or in holes and caves in the rocks. They catch mice, birds, hares, and other small animals, and they come to the farm-yard, and steal geese, ducks, turkeys, and chickens. The Fox takes the neck of a goose in his mouth, swings the body over his back, and runs swiftly to the woods, or to his hole to share it with his young ones. Foxes are hunted with dogs called fox-hounds. And the farmer, who has had his geese and young

turkeys and chickens stolen, sets traps for the
Foxes; but he does not often catch them, for they
are very cunning as well as sly, and can often
tell where the trap is, even when it is carefully
covered up with straw or leaves. Sometimes the
Fox outwits both the dogs and the hunters that
are pursuing it. A certain Fox was often chased
by dogs and hunters, but it always used to get
away from them at the same place, and the hunters could not understand it; but at last it was
found out that the Fox, being so far ahead of the
dogs and men that they could not see him, leaped
from a fallen log on to a very sloping tree,
up which he crawled till he was hidden by the
branches; there he would lie till the dogs and
hunters passed; then he would jump down and
run back to the thicket or tree-top from which
he first started. Foxes, when caught alive, often
pretend to be dead. A gentleman told me that
he once set a trap for a Fox so carefully that he
caught the sly animal. He set the trap just before night when it was snowing, and so his tracks
and the trap were covered over with snow. The
Fox came to get the bait, and stepped upon the

trap; it sprung, and caught the Fox by the leg.
The trap was not fastened, and so the Fox dragged
it some distance through the snow; the gentleman followed the track, and at last overtook the
Fox, and struck him with a little stick; at once
the Fox seemed to be dead; the gentleman took
him up and carried him home, his foot still in the
trap.   When he got home the Fox was perfectly
well, and if he had been taken from the trap when
first struck, and when he seemed to be dead, he
would have jumped up and run away in a moment.   There is a picture of a Fox, with the dogs,
on the thirty-ninth page.

The Civet.

This pretty little Civet lives in Texas and California, and it is about as large as a cat; its home
is on the trees, and it is very lively and playful, and so easily tamed that the miners often

keep it for a pet. Its tail is prettily marked with
black and white rings.

Weasels live in walls, in stone-heaps, under the
roots of old trees, and sometimes in cellars, and

The Weasel.

about old mills; they are very small and slender, with soft thick fur, which is brown in summer and white in winter, and the tail has a black
tip. The fur is called Ermine, and many years
ago was worn only by kings and nobles. The
best Ermine is brought from Siberia, a very cold
country in Asia. Weasels are very bold and bloodthirsty, and often kill animals much larger than
themselves. They destroy many chickens; one of
them killed fifty in two nights.

The Sable lives in the deep woods of the northern parts of our country; it catches and eats
hares, birds, and squirrels. In winter it makes
its home in a hollow tree, and the hunter often
sees it sitting with its head just out of its hole.
When so seen the hunter does not shoot it, for

it would fall back into its nest and be lost; but he walks slowly around the tree, the sable

The Sable.

comes out to look at him, and is then shot. Its fur is of a beautiful dark brown color, and is made into cloaks, collars, and muffs, and is often called Hudson Bay Sable. The costly Russian Sable fur comes from Siberia.

Sometimes in the winter you may see on the ice and snow of ponds and brooks, and about rivers, a little slender dark brown or black creature, smaller than a cat. It is the little Mink, which lives near the water, and has the dark, glossy, beautiful fur often called American Sable, which is made into so many warm garments for the winter. The Mink has its toes partly webbed, and it can swim and dive with ease; and when pursued it often takes to the water and swims away to some hiding-place. Sometimes when

closely followed by dogs it will climb a tree, but
it does not often do so unless chased. When
running and rambling about, it often stops, raises

The Mink.

itself upon its hind legs and listens, looks around,
and sniffs the air as if it were on the watch for
an enemy. It hunts its food mainly at night,
although it may be often seen running about in
the daytime ; and it is active all the winter. The
Mink digs a burrow in the ground, in which it
lives, and the end of the burrow is enlarged into
a sort of chamber, and in this chamber its little
nest is made. The nest is of a rounded shape,
with an opening on one side, and it is built of
dry soft grasses, and nicely lined with feathers.
In the woods, the burrows are often made under logs, or under the roots of trees near the

water; sometimes the burrows run along under rocks, or under stone walls. The Mink often saves the trouble of digging its burrow, by finding that of a muskrat, and, after driving out the owner, taking possession of the house and burrow, and keeping it for its own. This suits the Mink very well, as the muskrats' burrows always lead to the water. Sometimes the Mink lives in the hollow of a fallen tree, and sometimes in the old hollow roots of a tree which lie near the water. The Mink feeds wholly upon other animals, following them by scent as the dogs do, though when near its prey it often steals forward and springs upon it, like a cat. It eats small quadrupeds, grouse, quails, and water-birds and their eggs, and fishes, frogs, and other water animals. Sometimes the Mink takes up its abode near the farm-yard, under the barn or under a haystack, and in the night comes to the coop and steals the young turkeys and chickens. It is quite a brave little animal, and when attacked by dogs or muskrats, it fights with much courage and is not easily killed. It takes good care of its young while they are in the nest, but as soon as they are able to take care of themselves, they leave the mother, and before winter each one makes or finds a home for itself.

The Wolverine.

Here is a picture of a very powerful, fierce, and greedy animal, about the size of a large dog. It is the Wolverine, which lives in the cold regions of the North. It follows the sable-trappers, and troubles them by eating the game; and it is so shrewd and cunning that it will even spring the trap without getting caught itself, and then devour the bait.

You have often seen the soft, warm fur collars which gentlemen wear in winter, and you will like to know what animal has such pretty, thick fur. These collars are made of the skins of the Otter, a long, slender, beautiful animal which lives in and about ponds, rivers, and large brooks. Its food is fishes, and it can swim so fast beneath the water that it can catch even the swiftest of

The Otter.

them. Otters are very playful, and they love to " slide down hill " almost as well as you do. Their sliding-place is the steep, wet bank of a river, where, time after time, they slide down head foremost, going splash into the water at the bottom. They make their nest in the river's bank, and sometimes in a hollow tree or log; and they line it with dry grasses and leaves, so that it may be soft and warm for their little ones.

This pretty little black and white creature, with its long flowing hair, and its beautiful large bushy tail, is the Skunk, which is so much disliked foɪ

The Skunk.

its bad odor. It lives only in America, and for its home it digs a burrow in the ground, in which it stays during the daytime. It comes out at night, and feeds upon beetles and other little insects, and eggs, often stealing into the hen-coop to rob the nests, and sometimes to kill and eat the hens and little chickens.

The Badger lives in the western part of our

country. It is about the size of a small dog, and its body is very stout. Its fur is soft, fine, and silky, and on the hind part of the body it is so long as almost to hide its short tail. It feeds

The Badger.

upon mice and prairie squirrels, which it digs out of their holes, and it also eats young birds, eggs, and insects. It digs a dark and winding bur- row, in which it stays most of the day, and in this burrow it makes a warm nest of soft dry mosses and grass.

When white people first came to this country to make it their home, great forests covered almost the whole land, and in these forests lived many fierce, hungry animals, — the wolves, panthers or pumas, and the bears. Many of the great forests have been cut down, and the land is made into beautiful smooth green fields; but the mountains and the wild parts of our country are still covered with deep woods, in which some of these animals are still living. You have read about the puma, and the wolf, and you will like to know something about the bears. They are very large and powerful animals, with very long sharp claws; they live in caves, and in hollow trees, and eat other animals, and also berries, roots, nuts, acorns, and insects, and they are fond of green corn and honey. The Black Bear is common in the forests of our country, and although so large and strong it does not often attack man unless angry or in defence of its little ones. This Bear is very fond of ripe blackberries, and when it finds a nice cluster, it picks off each ripe berry, one by one, without touching the green ones or breaking the bushes.

The Grizzly Bear lives on the Rocky Mountains, and in California. It is much larger than the Black Bear, and it is the fiercest animal in our country, and so strong that it can kill and drag

The Grizzly Bear.

away the great bison or buffalo, an animal as large as an ox.

The Grizzly loves the woods and thickets, and he prowls about in search of food in the day-time as well as at night. His great tracks are often seen along the banks of the rivers, where he wanders to see what he can find to eat. Like the Black Bear, the Grizzly is fond of wild fruits and berries, and when these are ripe he goes in search of them, and he stands upright beside the bushes and small trees, and bends them over, or pulls them down, and then picks and eats the wild plums, and the berries which he likes so well. He sometimes comes out of the woods, and goes to the gardens near the forts, and there picks and eats the green peas. The Grizzly some-times attacks hunters and travellers, especially if he be hungry, or if the hunters have wounded him. Sometimes he suddenly springs upon a group of travellers and bears away one of their number, before there is time for any one to resist him.

There was once a party of men travelling in the wild regions where the Grizzly Bears live.

They had been rowing their canoe during the day, but when night came on, they landed, drew their boat out of the water upon the shore, and tilted it up behind them, and built a fire, and began to get their supper. While they were all seated around the fire, and enjoying the pleasant evening, a big Grizzly Bear leaped over the canoe, seized one of the men and quickly carried him off. All the men but one were much frightened. But one brave man grasped a gun and followed the bear, and saw him going farther and farther away with the man held fast in his mouth. He called out to the poor man who was in the bear's mouth, and told him that he was afraid to shoot, fearing that he would hit him instead of the bear; but the poor man called back to him, and told him to shoot at once, as the bear was squeezing him to death. So the brave man took good aim with his rifle, and sent a ball into the body of the bear; the bear immediately dropped the man, and ran after the one who had shot him, but the bear was wounded so severely that he could not overtake him, and so he went away into the woods and was seen no more. The man that was rescued from the bear was very badly bitten and hurt, but he at last got well.

The Polar or Great White Bear lives in the cold regions of the North. It makes its nest in the deep snow. You may think it strange that such a nest can be warm enough for baby bears; but the mother finds a nice place at the side of some large rock, and lies down, and the snow falls upon and covers her; the warmth of her body keeps the nest warm, and her breath makes a little hole in the snow above her, which lets in the pure air, and in this nest the old bear and the cubs, as the little ones are called, stay all winter. So you see that no animal need freeze to death if the snow is only deep enough to cover it.

The Raccoon.

The Raccoon looks very much like a little bear with a long tail. It lives in woods and near streams, for it likes to eat frogs, turtles' eggs, and mussels. It climbs trees and robs the nests of birds, and, when the corn is young and tender, comes at night into the cornfields to feast upon it. The nest is often made in a hollow tree. A young Raccoon is easily tamed, and becomes gentle and playful. Your papa has a friend who once kept one of these little animals as a pet for several months, and the little cunning fellow would go every morning to a basin of water, and wash his hands and face.

I think, Amy, you have not forgotten the pretty Seals which we saw in the large tank of sea-water

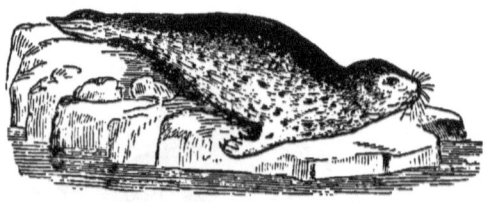

The Seal.

at the Aquarial Gardens in Boston. They were so tame that when their keeper called them by their names, Ned and Fanny, they would come to him, and, at his bidding, would shoulder a little musket, turn the crank of a hand-organ, shake hands with visitors, and Ned would even "throw a kiss" to the ladies. Seals live in the sea, and they have a head which looks like that of a dog; their eyes are large, dark, and very beautiful. Seals often crawl out of the water upon the rocks, and, in cold seas, upon the floating ice, to lie in the sunshine.

You may sometimes see a seal swimming in the sea, when you are going to Nahant by steamboat; but you will see only its head; it keeps its body below the surface of the water.

There are many kinds of Seals. Some kinds have a body no larger than that of a dog; others are very large; one kind is twenty or thirty feet in length. The people of Greenland, and of other cold and icy regions of the North, hunt these animals every day, and were it not for the Seals, they would starve and freeze; for the flesh of the Seal is their principal food: its fat gives them oil for their lamps, and for their fires, and they also eat it with their food; its skin is made into warm and strong garments, and it is also used to cover their boats, their sledges, and their tents, and it is cut into straps for their harness, and for

their whips ; its stomach is used for an oil flask ;
its sinews are used, instead of thread and silk,
for sewing; and its bones are made into hooks,
knives, and spear-points.   The Greenlander goes
in his seal-skin boat to hunt the Seals, and when
he gets near one he throws his harpoon into it ;
the Seal at once dives below the water, and when
it comes up again the man attacks it with his
lance and at last kills it.

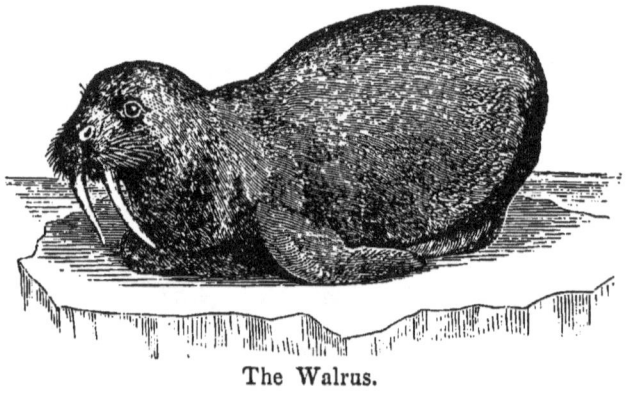

The Walrus.

The Walrus lives in the sea in the cold regions
of the North, and looks a little like a large seal,
but its " eye-teeth " are very long, forming two
stout tusks, as you see them in the picture.   The
Walruses use these tusks in climbing out of the
water on to the shore, or on to the ice-banks ;

and they also use them in tearing up sea-weeds and sea-shells, upon which they feed. The Walrus is as large as the largest ox you ever saw, and it is covered with short brown hair. Although it lives in the water, it likes to come upon the land and sleep in the warm sunshine. Large herds of these animals are often seen lying upon the rocks, or on the fields of ice. While the Walruses are sleeping, one of their number is awake and on the watch, and if he sees danger near, he awakes the others by a loud bellowing, and all plunge into the water as soon as they can. When upon the shore they are often attacked by the Polar bear, and they then fight very hard to defend themselves. Walruses are hunted for their oil, which is used in lamps, and for many other purposes, and they are also hunted for their tusks, which are good hard ivory, and are made into knife-handles and many other useful and beautiful articles. When attacked by the hunters they fight very fiercely, and they bravely defend their young ones. They can readily smash a boat in pieces with their tusks, or they can upset a boat by hooking their tusks over the sides of it.

THE PLANT-EATERS.

HERE is a picture of the Virginia Deer. You have seen this beautiful and graceful animal in the lovely gardens at Belmont, and in other places. Its little ones are called fawns. When wild it is

The Virginia Deer.

very timid, and if startled, it bounds over the plains and through the forest with great speed. But those that you have seen were very tame, and would come and eat the fresh, sweet clover from your hand.

In winter the Deer eats the buds of many kinds of shrubs, such as the wild rose, the hawthorn, the azalea, the winter-green, the partridge-berry, and many others; in summer it feeds upon the tender grasses, and it sometimes comes to the planters' grain-fields, and eats the young wheat, oats, and corn; it is also fond of berries; in autumn it eats the chestnuts and beechnuts, which fall upon the ground, and it also comes to the oak-trees to feed upon the acorns. The Deer is said to feed mainly at night, but in those places where it is not often disturbed, it may be seen feeding in the morning and in the afternoon. In the Southern and Middle States, the Deer sometimes come in the summer to the plantations and leap over the fences, and hide during the daytime in a thicket, or among the vines and briers, and at night feed upon the leaves and tender fruit of the growing plants; at other times they go four or five miles away to spend the day, often swimming rivers in their journeys to and from the feeding-grounds. In cold weather the Deer likes to rest during the day in some dry place, where it may be sheltered from the winds, and warmed by the sunshine. In warm weather it often rests in shady swamps, or among the bushes which grow near brooks and streams. During the warm months it is often much troubled by flies and mosquitoes, and to avoid them it lies down in the shallow water with only its antlers and a part of its head exposed. The Deer are very fond of water, and they go every night to some pond or stream to drink. They are also very fond of salt, and often go at the morning and evening twilight, or by moonlight, to the salt springs ; they do not seem to drink the water, but they lick the stones and the earth on the edges of the springs and streams. The Virginia Deer is hunted for its flesh, which is called venison, and which is very good for food.

Here is a picture of the great Moose, which lives in the cold parts of our country. It is the largest of all the Deer, being taller than a horse, and with very large, broad, and flat horns. Its legs are so long that it does not need to leap over fences and fallen trees, but steps over them with ease. In the summer it comes to the lakes and rivers to feed upon the water-plants, and to get away from the flies which are so troublesome at that time;

The Moose.

in the winter many of them stay in "yards"; these are large tracts of ground on which the snow has been trodden down hard by the Moose, the light, untrodden snow around the yard serving as walls. Here the Moose are quite safe, as wolves dare not enter.

Far away across the ocean, in the peat-bogs of Ireland, there have been found the bones of a deer much larger than the Moose or any other kind of deer now living on the earth. These bones belonged to a deer called the Great Irish Elk, which lived many thousand years ago. It was ten feet high to the top of its horns, and the tips of its broad horns were ten feet apart!

The Reindeer is much smaller than the Moose. It lives in cold regions, and is very hardy; in summer it eats the buds and twigs of shrubs, and in winter it scrapes the snow from the ground, and feeds upon a little plant called the " reindeer-moss."

This animal is very useful to the people that live in Lapland, who keep large herds of them, and use them as we use cattle and horses; their milk and flesh are good for food, their skins make warm clothing, their sinews are used for thread, and their horns are made into knives and other useful articles, and their tongues are luxuries which are sent to many parts of the world. The speed of the Reindeer is very great. In a palace

The American Reindeer, or Caribou.

in Sweden there is a painting of one which drew an officer, with important despatches, the distance of eight hundred miles in forty-eight hours.

The North American Reindeer is called Caribou. It lives in Maine and Canada, and westward to the region of Lake Superior, and as far north as Greenland.

Another very large deer is the Elk, or Wapiti, which lives in Pennsylvania, Michigan, and Min-

The Elk, or Wapiti.

nesota. It is about as large as the moose, and its horns are very long and very much branched. The horns of the Wapiti are sometimes so large that, when resting on their tips, a man can walk erect between them. All kinds of deer shed their horns, which are called antlers, every year, and they grow again to their full size in the course of a few months.

The Musk Deer.

The pretty little Musk Deer lives on the high mountains of Thibet, in Asia. It is about as large as a goat, and has no horns. Two of its upper teeth grow very long and look like tusks. The perfume called musk is obtained from this deer.

The Giraffe lives in Africa, and feeds upon the leaves and tender twigs of trees; and its neck is so long that it can easily reach those that grow twenty feet from the ground! Its color is yellow, spotted with light and dark brown, and its eyes are large, full, and lustrous. It does not shed

its horns, which are small and covered with a
hairy skin. When attacked by an animal from

The Giraffe.

which it cannot escape, the Giraffe defends itself
by kicking, and in this way it can sometimes
tire out and beat off even the fierce lion.

In the Western part of our country, on the mountains and on the plains, lives the beautiful Prong-horn Antelope. It is as large as a sheep, and has a long neck, and very long legs. Hundreds are sometimes seen together, and when

The Prong-horn Antelope.

alarmed they bound across the plains and along the slopes of the mountains with great swiftness. It is called Prong-horn because of the branch or prong which it has on each horn, and which you can see in the picture.

The Rocky Mountain Goat lives on the steep sides of the Rocky Mountains. It is as large as

a sheep, and looks very much like the common
goat. It has a coat of long white hair and thick

The Rocky Mountain Goat.

white wool, and its horns and feet are of a shining
black color. Although this animal looks like a
goat, and is called a goat, it is truly an Antelope.
But you will want to know the difference between
a Goat and an Antelope, and I will tell you, —
Goats, and Sheep too, have dull brown and angular
horns, while Antelopes have black and round or
rounded horns. You see now why we call the
animal whose picture I here show you an Antelope.

Far away in Africa and in Arabia lives the small, graceful Gazelle, famous for its large, dark, and beautiful eyes. It is a very wild and timid little creature, but if caught when young, it can

The Gazelle.

be tamed, and then its beauty and its playfulness make it a charming pet. It runs faster than the swiftest greyhound, and sometimes large herds of a thousand or more are seen bounding over the plains together.

The little Chamois lives on the Alps, high mountains in Europe. It cannot endure heat, and in summer is found only on the snowy sides of the mountains, or in deep cold glens, where the snow, upon which it loves to lie, does not melt.

It is very shy, and at the least alarm bounds swiftly away over rocks, and up and down the steepest places, often springing upon a rock just

The Chamois.

large enough to hold its four feet placed close together.

To shoot the Chamois the hunters toil very hard, and go into very dangerous places. The chamois-hunter starts from home in the night, so that he can get to the places where the Chamois are to be found very early in the morning, even before these animals come forth to feed. When he gets near the place where he thinks he shall find his game, he looks all about with a telescope. If he does not see any of the Chamois, he goes farther up the mountain, until he sees one of these beautiful animals, and then he goes far around, keeping behind the rocks, so as to get above the Chamois before it sees him; and at last he gets near enough to shoot it. When he has shot the Chamois he quickly goes to it, and lifts it upon his shoulder, and carries it down the rugged mountain and home to his family.

It is very difficult to get near the Chamois when there are many together, for while they are feeding one of their number is always on the look-out, and when it sees any danger it warns them, and they all bound away together, over rocks, snows, and glaciers; and the hunter, if he would get one of them, must toil on for hours and hours, and travel miles and miles in the most difficult and dangerous places. Sometimes night comes on while he is following the Chamois, but the hunter is not discouraged; he travels on as long as he can see, and then he finds some place where he may lie down beside a rock and spend the night. He eats his supper of bread and cheese, which he has brought with him in his bag, and then goes to sleep, with only a stone for his pillow. In the morning he is up very early, and after eating a scanty breakfast he starts off again to try and find his game ; and thus he sometimes spends two or three days alone on the mountains.

The Mountain Sheep.

The Mountain Sheep, or Big-horn, lives on the slopes of the Rocky Mountains. It is very much larger than the common sheep, and its horns are very large and strong. The hunters say that this sheep sometimes leaps from very high places, and, falling head-foremost, strikes upon the tips of its great strong horns, receiving no injury.

Here is a picture of the Musk Ox, that lives far away in the cold regions of the North; its dark brown silky hair is very thick and long,

The Musk Ox.

for in those icy places the animals need warm coats of hair, fur, or feathers, and God in his love and goodness has thus clothed them. The Musk Ox is very agile, and climbs up the steep sides of hills where the snow has been blown away by the winds, and feeds upon the grasses, mosses, and lichens which grow there.

The Bison, or Buffalo, is the largest animal in America, being as large as an ox. It lives in large herds on the plains far beyond the Mississippi

The Bison or Buffalo.

River. Buffaloes are hunted for their skins, which are made into the buffalo-robes that keep us warm when we ride in the cold winter. Sometimes the plains are covered with these animals as far as the eye can reach, and travellers have passed through great herds of them for days and days, without their numbers seeming to grow less; and their paths look more like great travelled roads, than like the marks of hoofs. Buffaloes were

once common in the Eastern part of the United
States, even to the shores of the Atlantic ocean;
but they have been hunted and killed till now
none are found except far away in the West;
and I fear that by and by they and the Moose
and the Wapiti, and some others of the large animals of our country, will all be gone.

The Llama lives on the Andes, — high, cold
mountains in South America. It is much larger

The Llama.

than a sheep, and is covered with long, soft hair
of a brown or gray color. It is tamed by the
people of the regions in and near which it lives,
and it is used to carry burdens from place to

place. The wild Llamas are hunted for their flesh, and also for their skins. The people of Peru use the dried flesh of the Llama for food, and the skins of one kind, called the Alpaca, are very highly prized, for the hair is very fine, long, and silky, and it is made into beautiful and costly cloths. The Llamas drink very little water, but they like to feed upon juicy plants. They eat a sort of rush-like grass which grows upon the mountains, and they also eat the mosses and lichens which grow upon the rocks. Their native haunts are in and near the regions where snow and hail often fall, and they cannot well bear the heat for a long time. They carry easily about one hundred pounds in weight, and if treated kindly they are very good-natured; but if they get provoked, they turn and spit at the person who offends them. When not using them, their masters allow them to graze upon the mountains, and the tame Llamas are often seen grazing in the same pastures with the wild ones. And if the wild Llamas get frightened and run, the tame Llamas do not run too, as you might suppose they would, but they seem to like to be near man, and never run away to get their freedom again.

The Camel looks a little like the Llama, but it is very much larger, being larger than a horse, and it stands very high. There are two kinds of Camel; one kind has two humps upon its back; the other has only one hump. The home of the Camel is in Africa and Asia, and it is formed

The Camel.

for living on, and travelling over, the rocky and sandy deserts of those countries. It has always been so useful to the people in carrying burdens across the wide sandy plains, that it has often

been called the " ship of the desert." The feet
of the Camel are large and wide, and on the bottom of them are pads or cushions, which help
the Camel to tread firmly upon the soft, yielding
sands; and these cushions render the Camel's
tread so noiseless, that if one of these large animals were walking close beside you, even upon
rough and rocky ground, you could not hear its
footsteps. The cushions are covered with a hard
skin, which is not injured by the heated and almost
burning sands of the desert. The eyes of the Camel
are shielded from the light and the glare of the
sun by a large overhanging brow, and by very
long lashes to the eyelids; and the Camel, when
it wishes, can close its nostrils so as to keep out
the fine, driving sand which is raised by even the
slightest wind. Its stomach is formed to retain
a portion of the water which the animal drinks,
so that the Camel can easily go four or five days —
and sometimes it goes nine or ten days — without
drinking; and thus it can travel from well to
well, even though the wells, or drinking-places,
may be several hundred miles apart. It eats the
coarsest herbs, and thorny shrubs, such as scarcely

any other animal will touch, and the leaves and branches of trees; and it also eats beans, dates, and cakes of barley. It can live for many days upon very little food, but when obliged to do this, its hump becomes smaller, for the fat of which it is composed is, at such times, taken back into the system to nourish the Camel and keep it alive. After a long and painful journey, when the supply of food has been scanty, the Camels arrive with backs almost straight, instead of the great hump, or humps, which are natural to them; and it often takes months of rest, and much good food, to put the Camels in good condition to travel again. The Camel is good-natured, and willing to share its food with other animals; and it is very gentle and patient, and even when overloaded it will not refuse to rise, and when weary it will not refuse to move on. The Camel is so tall that it is taught to kneel to receive its load, and to have its load taken off. When the Camel rests, and sleeps, it kneels and rests upon its breast. On its breast and on its legs are hard callous spots; and upon these the weight of the body comes when the Camel kneels and rises. When it rises it lifts its hind feet first, and a person who is then upon its back, and who is not used to sitting and riding upon the Camel, is in danger of being thrown forward over the animal's head.

For thousands of years these animals have been used by the people of Egypt, Arabia, Persia, and other Eastern countries, for carrying travellers and goods from one region or place to another; they have also been used in war, and it was the custom of some nations, when they went to battle, to adorn their Camels with collars and chains of gold.

The merchants of the East often travel in large companies, loading many Camels with goods, and others with the food which will be needed on the long journey. These large companies of men and Camels are called caravans; and the number of Camels in a caravan is often many hundreds, and sometimes even several thousand. It was to the men of a caravan that Joseph was sold by his brothers; this caravan was made up of Ishmaelites, Midianites, and Medanites, with their Camels, on their way to the markets of Egypt.

The Camels of a caravan are sometimes placed

in a single file, and they travel one after another ; at other times they travel side by side, presenting a broad front, a mile or more in extent. The caravans are often led by the sound of a bell, and when the music of the bell stops, all the Camels stop. Like many other animals, the Camels are fond of musical sounds, and when they are very tired, and almost ready to sink under their burdens, the drivers sing some cheering, lively melody, and the poor weary creatures brighten up, and move on more briskly towards the halting-place. They stop and rest at noon ; and at night the Caravan halts, and the Camels are unloaded. If the weather is very hot the caravan moves only at night, starting at eight o'clock in the evening, and going on till after midnight. The camel-drivers always stop near shrubs and bushes, if they can, so that the Camels may feed upon them. As there is no danger that the Camels will wander away to any great distance, and as they usually keep close to the spot where they are set at liberty, they are not often tied in any way. When they rest for the night, they almost always kneel in the form of a circle, and the men sleep in the centre of the circle. Unless the night is rainy, the men do not use a tent, but sleep upon the ground, the stars shining down upon them. A gentleman was walking, one dark night, near a little village a few miles from Smyrna, when he stumbled and fell over something which proved to be a young Camel, and getting up and going on he stumbled again, and this time he fell over among a company of camel-drivers, for he had come upon the resting-place of a small caravan.

When the number of travellers is large, a great deal of water is needed for drinking, cooking, washing, and bathing, and the Camels carry a supply to be used for these purposes. The water is carried in leather bags or bottles, called water-skins. Sometimes many Camels are loaded only with water, but usually each Camel carries one water-skin in addition to its other load. The air in the desert regions is so dry and hot that the men are often very thirsty, but the custom is to drink only at stated and regular times, and the caravan halts for that purpose. The men and Camels often suffer greatly on these long marches. Sometimes the winds that blow are so hot that

the water in the water-skins is partly or wholly
dried up. Sometimes clouds of fine sand fill the
air; then the traveller gets down beside his Camel,
closes his eyes, and wraps his cloak about his
head, and waits till the sand-cloud passes. The
Camels scent water at a great distance; and when
all are suffering from the want of water, and the
drivers do not know where to turn to find it, they
let their Camels take their own course, knowing
that if there is water in that region they will
find it.

Besides the merchant caravans, there are the
pilgrim caravans, which are much larger, and
contain thousands and thousands of people, and
many thousand Camels. These caravans go from
different parts of Asia and Africa to Mecca.
Mecca is an old city in Arabia, where a man
named Mohammed was born, and where he wrote
a book called the Koran, which the Mohammedans,
or followers of Mohammed, read and believe, as
we read and believe our blessed Bible. The Mohammedans go to Mecca to worship. Four of
these great caravans go to Mecca every year;
one of them starts from Cairo, one from Damascus,

one from Babylon, and one from Zibith, a town near the Red Sea. You can look upon the maps of Africa and Asia, and see where these places are marked, and when you are older you will learn about them.

Here is a picture of the Elephant, the largest animal that lives upon the land. Its home is in Asia and Africa, where it is often seen in large herds. It is covered with a tough, hard skin, which is almost always of a dark gray color, but sometimes the skin is white. The nose of the Elephant is very long, and is called a trunk, and is used to carry food and water to the mouth. At the end of the trunk there is a sort of finger, with which the Elephant can easily pick up very small articles, and the keepers of tame ones train them to pick up pennies, and even needles, to amuse those who come to see them. Its food is the leaves and branches of trees, and large juicy plants. Two of its teeth grow into enormous tusks; and from these tusks comes the ivory that is used for combs, knife-handles, chessmen, and many other useful and beautiful articles. Many thousands of these tusks are brought to England every year. The Elephant uses these large tusks to drive off his enemies, and to root up small

The Elephant.

trees, and to break down the branches of large ones, either to feed upon the leaves, or to make a passage for his huge body through the thick forests. When not teased, the tame Elephant is mild and gentle, but if provoked he does not fail to revenge himself.

A man once went to see a tame Elephant, taking with him a package of nice ginger-cakes, and also 'a package of cakes hot with ginger and pepper, and while looking at the animal he gave him some of the nice cakes to eat, for which the Elephant seemed to be very grateful. By and by the man took from his pocket the package of cakes hot with ginger and pepper, and gave the whole package to the Elephant, and the Elephant took the package in his trunk, carried it to his mouth, and, after chewing it, swallowed the whole. As soon as he had swallowed the peppery cakes, he gave a loud roar, and appeared to suffer greatly, and, with his trunk, gave the water-bucket to his keeper, in that way showing that he wanted water to drink; the water being brought he drank six pailfuls, carrying the water to his mouth in his trunk; and he was so angry with the man who gave him the peppery cakes, that as soon as he had finished drinking, he hurled the bucket at the man with such force, that, if it had hit him, it would have killed him. A year afterward the same man went again to see the same Elephant, and carried good and bad cakes as before. He first gave the Elephant some good cakes; then he offered him a bad one, and as soon as the Elephant tasted it, he caught the man with his trunk, lifted him from the ground, swung him around, tore off part of his coat, seized the pockets and eat all the good cakes, trampling the bad ones under his feet; then he tore the coat in pieces, and threw the pieces, and the fragments of the bad cakes at the man who had offended him.

Elephants are trained to do many kinds of useful work in the countries where they live; they draw heavy loads, carry heavy baggage on their backs, carry timber on their tusks, and with their trunks and tusks pile up logs and wood for their masters.

In India, the Elephant is used in hunting wild animals, the hunters riding to the chase upon the Elephants' backs; and many years ago it was much more used than now. The princes and rich men of India once kept very large herds of Elephants for the use of themselves and their friends; and when one of these princes or rich men went upon a hunting excursion, he made it as grand an affair as he could. I will tell you about one of these rich princes, and the way he went a hunting. His name was Asoph-ul-doulah, and he lived in a palace at the city of Lucknow. He used to go to the hunt early in the spring of the year, in March; and he sometimes took with him ten thousand armed men on horses, ten thousand armed men on foot, eight hundred elephants, and from forty to sixty thousand persons, called camp-followers, and who carried along food, and goods, or merchandise. This large army used to start from Lucknow, and the prince himself, mounted on an Elephant, rode in the centre of the line; and on each side of him was another Elephant for his own use; one of these was intended specially for the chase when he should get to the hunting-grounds. On his right, and on his left, was a long rank of Elephants. On and on they moved; the Elephants and their riders, the horsemen, the footmen, and the camp-followers, trampling down the grass, flowers, bushes, and the fields of grain that were in their path. At last they reached the hunting-grounds; a camp was formed, tents were pitched; and for weeks and weeks all kinds of wild animals were hunted and killed.

The Elephant is the only animal that can be ridden in the tiger-hunt; horses and camels are so afraid of tigers, they cannot be used at all for this purpose. The scent of the Elephant is so keen that he knows when he is near a tiger, even when the beast is hidden in the thick jungle; and when he finds himself near one of these powerful and ferocious wild beasts, he is very uneasy, and holds his trunk very high up, so that the tiger cannot spring upon it, and tear and wound it. If the tiger attack him, he tries to get the tiger under his feet so as to crush him. Sometimes the Elephant catches him upon his tusks and tosses him high in the air, or throws him violently to a great distance. Sometimes the Elephant plunges forward, and with his tusks pierces through the tiger, and pins him to the ground, killing him upon the spot.

You will like to know how wild Elephants are caught, and I will tell you. In the regions where the Elephants live, the Elephant-catchers make a large, strong pen of beams and logs of wood, the upright parts being set very deep in the ground, so as to stand firmly. From the large pen there is an opening into a smaller one, and from this into another still smaller. After the pens are all ready, many hundred men surround a large herd of Elephants, and begin to drive them toward the pens. As Elephants are very much afraid of fire, the men build fires at night, and these keep the Elephants from trying to get out of the ring which the men have formed around them. In the daytime the men make a great noise with guns and drums, and so the Elephants are driven nearer and nearer the pens, and at last they are driven into the large pen, and then the entrance to it is at once tightly closed; then they are driven forward into the next pen, and then into the smallest one of all. From the smallest pen there is a long narrow passage, just large enough for one Elephant at a time to pass along. Into this passage the Elephants, one by one, are driven, or coaxed by food, and are then bound with strong ropes; a strong rope is also put around the neck of each Elephant, and each end of the rope is fastened to a well-trained tame Elephant, and thus the tame Elephant helps his master to take the captured one to two large trees, to both of which he is securely fastened, — the Elephant standing between the two. The Elephant at first roars and struggles, and tries hard to get away; but soon he becomes tired out, and weak, and hungry, and he is willing to eat the food which is brought to him; and so he grows tamer and tamer every day, and by and by he comes to like the man who brings him food, and obeys him as his master.

A great many years ago Elephants were used in war, the soldiers fighting from towers which these animals carried upon their backs.

In the bottom of the peat-bogs, and in some other places, in our country, there are found the bones of an animal which lived many thousand years ago, and which was much like the Elephant, but very much larger, and its teeth were not flat on the crown like those of the Elephant. It is called the Mastodon, and was once as common perhaps in the United States as Elephants are now in Africa and Asia.

THE WHALES.

You remember, Amy, the White Whale which we saw in a tank of sea-water at the Aquarial

The White Whale.

Gardens in Boston; and how he would swim around and around his tank, and every few minutes come to the top of the water to breathe. He was so tame that he would come and take food from his keeper's hand; and he was trained to a sort of harness, and drew a young lady in a shell-shaped boat placed in the tank. This Whale was caught in the Gulf of St. Lawrence, and packed in wet sea-weeds, and brought to Boston, then lifted into the great tank where we saw him, and where he seemed to feel as much at home as if he were in the ocean, where he was born.

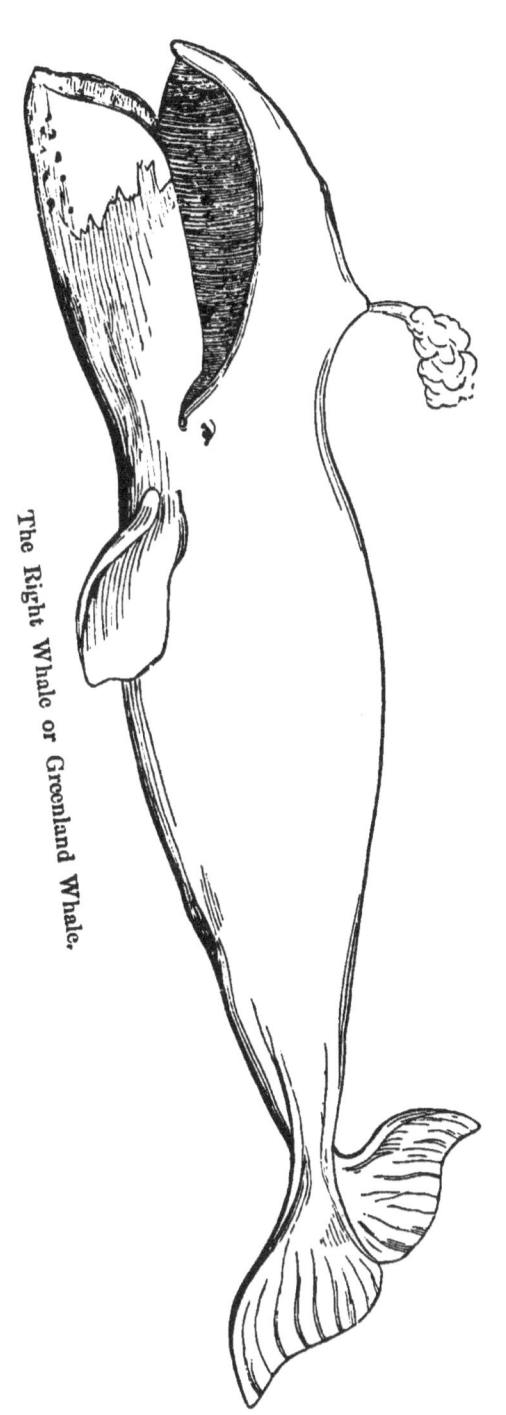

The Right Whale or Greenland Whale.

Some kinds of Whales are very large, — the largest animals in the world. On the previous page there is a picture of one of the large ones. It is called the Right Whale. It lives in the cold parts of the ocean, and its food is very small sea-animals, for it has no teeth, and so cannot crush the bones of large fishes; but hanging down from the upper jaw are rows, or slabs, of whalebone, which are very much split and fringed on the inside. When the Whale is hungry, he opens his enormous mouth and takes in thousands and thousands of the little sea-animals at once, and all the water that he takes in with them is strained off through this fringed whalebone, and every little animal remains in his mouth and is swallowed.

The Whalebone.

Here is a picture of the head of this Whale, with

the skin and flesh taken off, so as to show the whalebone in the position in which it grows.

You have often seen pieces of it; for it is this whalebone which is used in dresses, umbrellas, &c. It is often called *baleen*. The slabs are eight or ten feet long in a large Whale.

Another large kind is called the Sperm Whale. It has no whalebone, but has teeth in its lower

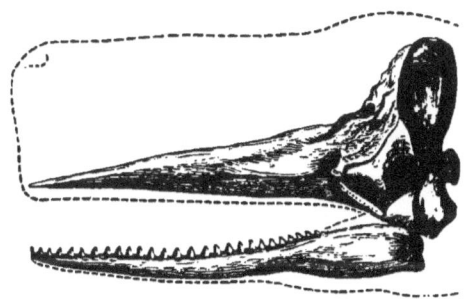

The Head of the Sperm Whale.

jaw. A few years ago, before the oil-wells in Pennsylvania and other parts of our land were known, many ships were employed, and many men were busy in pursuing and killing these large Whales; for at that time the oil in our lamps came from these animals. From the head of the Sperm Whale comes the spermaceti, which is used in making nice white candles. The sailors dip the oil with large buckets, and fill many barrels from the head of one Whale. The very costly substance called ambergris is found in the Sperm Whale. It is used in making perfumery, and it has the power, when mixed with other perfumes, of making them more intense. It is very light, and is often found floating on the water where one of these animals has died.

From our country alone, about seven hundred vessels and nearly twenty thousand men have been sent out, in a single year, to pursue and capture Whales. As soon as the vessels reach the "whaling-grounds," or those parts of the ocean where these animals are found, a constant watch for the Whales is kept from the mast-head of each vessel, and when one of these great creatures is seen, the "lookout" — as the man who is watching is called — cries, "There she blows! There she blows!" Then the captain orders the boats lowered and manned, and everything is soon made ready for the pursuit. The Whale when first seen is sometimes miles away from the ship, and often the man on the watch sees only the blowing, or spouting of the Whale. I must tell you about

this, and also how the sailors can tell a Right
Whale from a Sperm Whale, when it is many
miles away. Although the Whales live in the
water, they breathe air, and must often come to
the surface to get a supply of it. The Right
Whale has, on the top of the hind part of his
head, two openings, called " blow-holes "; through
these he breathes, and also from these he spouts
out water which has been taken into his great
mouth; and this stream of water, mingled with
the warm, moist breath of his lungs, comes out
of these openings with such force that it often
rises to the height of thirty, forty, or even fifty
feet, and can be seen at a great distance. When
its power is spent, and it begins to fall, part of
the water falls upon one side, and part on the
other; and so when the sailors see a whale spouting in this way they know that it is a Right Whale.
The Sperm Whale has only one opening, or blow-
hole, and it does not spout water, but only the
warm moist breath from the lungs; and this looks
like a white mist, and soon fades away.

Every whaling vessel carries from four to eight
boats; for, in order to capture the Whales, they

must be chased until the men get near enough to
them to throw harpoons into them, and to strike
and wound them with their lances; the Whale
is attacked with both these weapons. The harpoon is a long shaft of iron, with a flat, broad
head which tapers to a point, and which is sharp-
ened on both edges. The harpoon is attached to
a long, stout line, and so when the Whale is
struck by a harpoon, he is "fast," as the sailors
say. The rope to which the harpoons are fastened
is very long, and to keep it from getting tangled
it is kept nicely coiled in tubs. The tubs of rope
are placed near the middle of the boat, and the
rope passes from the tub to the stern of the boat,
and around a post, which is firmly fixed to the
framework of the boat; from this post the rope
leads along the whole length of the boat, to the
bow where it passes out through a notch. When
the boat is near enough to the Whale, the harpooner throws the harpoon with such force that
it often sinks deep into the body of the Whale.
The Whale feels the cold sharp iron, and in its
fright and pain begins to "run," and moves
swiftly through the water, pulling out the line

so fast, that if it were not kept wet where it passes around the post, it would soon get on fire. Sometimes the rope gets tangled, and then there is great danger to the one who tries to untangle it; for if the rope gets a turn around the arm, or leg, the limb is torn off, or the poor man is pulled out of the boat and carried far down into the sea. I will tell you a story of a man who was drawn out of a boat in this way. The rope, which a Whale was taking out very swiftly, got tangled, and the man who sat near the post saw it, but had only time enough to slip the rope off the post and the tangled part was in a moment at the bow, where the captain was sitting; the captain was seen to stoop to clear it, and then he was gone; the boat-steerer seized a hatchet and chopped off the line, hoping, that when the captain felt the rope slacken, he would be able, though far below the surface of the water, to get himself away from it. The crew were so frightened that they could not speak a word. Several minutes passed, and then, when they were just beginning to give up all hope, the body of the captain rose to the top of the water, a little way from the boat, and the men, rowing forward, soon reached him and lifted him into the boat. At first he showed no sign of life, but shortly they saw that he breathed, and they quickly pulled for their ship, and put him on board, and tenderly cared for him, and in a few days he was well again. The captain, in telling the story, says that he was caught by the rope around his left wrist, and thus dragged swiftly through the water; with his right hand he tried to reach the knife in his belt, so as to cut the rope, but the force and pressure of the water kept his right arm pressed against his side. But at last he felt the rope slacken, and he seized his knife, and when the rope tightened again he pressed it with the edge of the knife, and cut it, and he knew nothing more till he found himself in the boat, in the care of his men.

The Whale often takes out several thousand feet of line, sometimes all that there is in the boat; and a man stands ready with a hatchet to cut the rope when there is danger that the boat will be pulled under the water by the Whale. When the Whale is running, the oarsmen row,

so as to keep up with him, and to be near enough
when he stops, to throw more harpoons, or to
attack him with the lances. These are sharp spears
of iron, which are plunged into the Whale when
the boat can get near enough for the men to use
them. But the boat must be kept out of reach
of the tail and fins of the Whale, for with one
stroke it can smash a boat in pieces, and sad acci-
dents have often happened in this way. But
usually several boats are lowered from the vessel
at the same time, to go in pursuit of a Whale,
and they keep near together, and if one is smashed,
or upset, the crew can be picked up by the other
boats, and thus saved from drowning. I have
read a story of some whalers who were cruising
for Whales in the Pacific Ocean. There were only
three boats attached to their ship. One day,
early in the morning, a Whale was seen, and
two of the boats were sent to capture it; they
were soon fast to the Whale, which darted off
and drew the boats far away over the waters,
out of sight of the ship. Not long after, another
Whale rose in the water, very near the ship, and
the captain ordered the one boat that was

left to be lowered, and leaving only one man and two boys in the ship, he sprang into the boat and with his crew started for the Whale. In a short time they had struck the Whale with their harpoons, and were swiftly carried about fifteen miles from the ship. The Whale then plunged down into the ocean, and they soon saw him far down in the clear water, rushing up, his great jaws open, to destroy the boat. By quickly sheering the boat to one side, the Whale missed his aim, and thrusting his huge head into the air, fell over on his side, and plunged into the water, and again rushed up to attack the boat, and this time also the crew managed to avoid the blow. The Whale went down the third time, and rose just under the boat, threw it high in the air, and the men and the broken boat were floating on the waves, so far from the ship that they could not be seen from its deck.   They knew not where the other boats were, and it seemed to them that they could only cling to the pieces of the boat for a little while, and then be lost in the sea. It was just noon; and all the long afternoon they floated on the waves. When the ship rose on the

billows they could just get a glimpse of her spars.
The sun set and night began to close in, and just
then they saw, far away, one of the boats going
back to the ship. They shouted, but the boat
kept on ; again they raised a shout, but the boat
still kept on; almost frantic with despair, they
shouted once more, and this time the boatmen
rested on their oars ; once more they shouted,
and the boat was seen to turn in pursuit, and
these poor men who had been struggling in the
water so many hours were soon lifted into the
boat, and carried almost lifeless to the ship. Once
when a Whale was chased by a boat, he suddenly
turned and made directly for his pursuers, and
they were so anxious to strike him that they
rushed on, and the boat soon struck the Whale's
head ; the oarsmen were knocked from their seats,
but the harpooner had time to throw his two
irons, and the Whale rolled over on his back with
his mouth open. Just then a wave struck the
boat and threw it into the Whale's mouth ; all
the men sprang out, and had just time to get
clear of the boat before it was crushed by the
Whale's great jaws. The crew were all picked

up by another boat which was near, and were thus saved from drowning.

Sometimes a Whale is killed by the harpoons in a few hours, at other times it is many hours before the Whale can be killed and towed to the ship. Several boats were once sent from a ship to capture a Whale which was seen far away in the water. After rowing four or five hours, the Whale was struck by the harpoons from one of the boats, and soon several more harpoons from the other boats were thrown into the Whale; the great animal rushed on, dragging the boats, and the men could not get near enough to strike with the lance; for as soon as they came near in order to strike, it would dive down into the water. The captain steered his ship in the direction the Whale and boats had gone, but it was all day and all night, and till the afternoon of the next day, before a line attached to the Whale could be secured on board the ship, and then the Whale dragged the ship for nearly two hours; and it was not till forty hours after the Whale was struck that it was killed. Sometimes when the Whale is struck it at once dives far down into the water, and with such force and fury that it has been known to break the bones of its head by striking many hundred feet below on the bottom of the sea.

When the Whale is dead it is towed to the ship, and fastened alongside by means of ropes and chains, and then begins the work of cutting it up, and trying out the oil, and stowing it away. Large pieces are cut from the Whale, and by means of great iron hooks and ropes are lifted on board the vessel, and lowered into a room, where they are cut into smaller pieces; these small pieces are then pitched upon deck, and are there cut and chopped so as to render them easy to be tried. On the deck of the vessel, firmly set in brick-work, are two or three great pots for trying out the oil. Each of these pots is large enough to hold several barrels. When ready to begin this work, the fires are lighted, a little oil is put in each pot, and then they are filled with the pieces of " blubber," as the fatty portions of the Whale are called. The men are now all busy; some are cutting the pieces for the kettles; others are putting pieces into the kettles;

some are feeding the fires with the scraps which
are skimmed out, — for after the fire is kindled, no
fuel is needed except the scraps from the kettles;
some are dipping the hot oil into a copper tank,
where it cools, and others are filling casks from
the tank and stowing them away in the ship.
The fires are kept up, and the work goes on, day
and night, until the Whale has been all cut in
pieces and the oil all tried out.   Each Whale
yields from seventy to three hundred barrels of
oil, according to its size and fatness.

Sharks and other fishes are often seen near the
ship, and about the body of the Whale, while it
is being cut up, and many hundred sea-birds also
come to feed upon the fragments.

Whales sometimes sink as soon as they are
killed, and this is very discouraging to the men
who have been chasing them, and trying so hard
to capture them; but when the men see that
the dead Whale is going down, they must quickly
cut all the ropes which hold it to the boat, or
the boat would be drawn under the water, and
all the men would be drowned.

Whales have been known, in their rage and

fury, to attack the ship itself, and, by knocking a hole in its bottom, cause it to sink. A ship named Essex, which sailed from Nantucket nearly fifty years ago, was destroyed in this way. A huge Sperm Whale rose in the water only a little way from the ship, and, swimming towards it, struck the bows such a blow that the vessel shook like a leaf; the Whale went down, passed under the ship, and soon appeared, lashing the sea with his tail and fins; he seemed to be hurt, and frantic with rage; he swam away from the ship, then turned and made directly for it, striking it again in the bows, this time making a large hole; the vessel began to sink, and the crew took to their boats, and for many days were exposed upon the sea in their open boats. At last they reached a low island, and there they landed and remained about a week. They then prepared to start for the island of Juan Fernandez, which was two thousand miles away; but three of the men preferred to remain on the little island; these have never since been heard from. The boats, three in number, started off, and nearly two months afterward the mate's boat, with only three living men, was taken up by an English vessel, and a few days afterwards the captain's boat was found, with two men in her, by an American vessel. These were all that were left out of a crew of twenty.

The Dolphins are whale-like animals which live together in the ocean, in large numbers. They are very lively, and often follow ships for several days, frolicking and sporting all the while, and

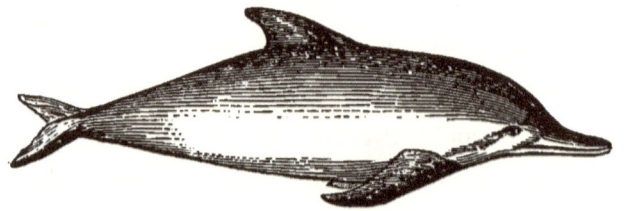

The Dolphin.

sometimes leaping so high out of the water as to fall upon the deck of the ship. The people who lived many years ago believed them to be very fond of music. The Dolphins, Porpoises, and Grampuses are animals which are much alike, and are often seen near each other.

In another book I shall show you the picture of a very beautiful fish which is also called Dolphin. So you see that this name is given to two animals which are very different from one another.

THE BATS.

IF you go to walk in summer, just as the soft evening twilight approaches, you will be almost sure to see a little animal flying above and around you, flitting and turning, now skimming along

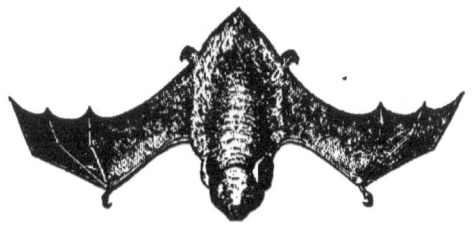

The Bat.

near the ground, now far above your head; you will only see him, you will not hear him, for his flight is very light and noiseless; you may think this is his play-time, and that he is only sporting; but this is his meal-time, and he is eating little insects, which he is catching every time he turns. Perhaps you will say it is a bird, but several times this summer the same little animal, or one of his cousins, has come in at our window, and after flying around the room several times, has suddenly alighted; and now he does not look at all like a bird, but like a little brown bunch of fur. It is a Bat, and he flies by means of a fine thin skin, which spreads out on each side of his body, from his neck to his hind legs, and to the ends of his long fingers. His little body is covered with soft thick fur; his eyes are very small, his ears are large, and on his thumb there is a sharp hook. In the daytime he sleeps in a cave, a hollow tree, or any other dark place, hanging by the sharp claws of his hind feet. In cold countries Bats sleep all winter.

THE INSECT-EATERS.

On the trees of Borneo, and other islands of the Indian Ocean, there lives a very curious animal, which looks a little like a bat, and which has a fine thin skin on the sides of its body, reaching from its fore feet to its hind ones. But it cannot fly like the bat; it can only take long leaps, this skin helping to support it in the air. It is called the Galeopithecus. During the day it is quiet, staying in the deep woods, but at night it is very nimble, running about on the

The Galeopithecus.

trees, and leaping from one tree to another in search of its food, which is fruits, insects, eggs, and birds.

You know how small and soft the mice are, but

The Shrew.

The Water Shrew.

here are two little creatures that are smaller than the smallest mouse you ever saw, and their fur is very soft and silky; they are Shrews. They live in meadows and fields, under rubbish, and heaps of stone, in old walls, and in holes in the ground. They make a warm nest of soft dry grasses and mosses, and their food is insects and worms. Some kinds live in the banks of streams, and swim about in the water, and feed upon little water-animals. These are called Water-Shrews.

When walking in the meadows, fields, or garden, you sometimes see little hills of loose earth just raised above the surface of the ground; they are called mole-hills, and here is a picture of the

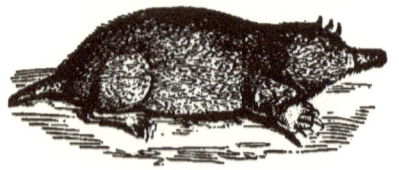

The Mole.

little Mole which makes them. It is about the size of a small rat; its body is very stout, and its fore feet are very large and fitted for digging. Its eyes are so small that many people think it has none; its fur is soft and thick, and feels like velvet, and every hair is so glossy that, although it lives and digs in the ground, no animal is cleaner than the little Mole. Its home is a winding burrow, in one part of which the nest is made, and from this part of the burrow lead many paths and galleries, so that, if the Mole is pursued, it is almost sure to escape. Another kind of Mole, about as large as this one, has a long nose, which at the end is shaped like a star; this one is 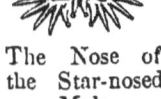 called the Star-nosed Mole.

The Nose of the Star-nosed Mole.

You will like to know something about the next two animals, although they do not live in America. The one called Tenrec lives on the island of Madagascar, the larger one is found in Europe. They are Hedgehogs, and they have, on the back, very sharp spines, and when alarmed

The Madagascar Hedgehog or Tenrec.

they curl themselves up, and this tightens the skin so much that the spines stand out on all sides, so that the bravest animal dares not attack them. They live in the hedges, and spend the

The European Hedgehog.

day in sleep, coming out at night for their food, which is fruits, roots, and insects.

THE GNAWERS.

ALL little folks like to watch the nimble and graceful little squirrels, which run and leap about on the trees and on the ground, and always seem to be so happy and so busy. They are very pretty too, with their large bright eyes and their great soft bushy tail. In the woods they eat nuts and acorns, and they come into the fields to get corn and grain. In winter these pretty little creatures live in hollow trees, where they make snug and warm nests. If disturbed before the young ones

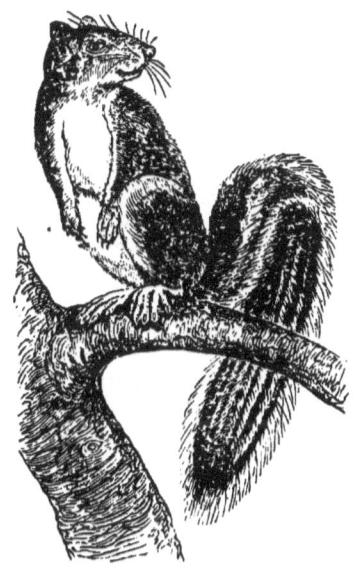

The Gray Squirrel.

are old enough to run and take care of themselves, the mother takes them in her mouth, one by one, and leaps away to a place of safety. A summer and autumn nest is built in the branches of a tree, and is made of twigs, leaves, and grasses. The Gray Squirrels are very beautiful, and they are often hunted for their skins; those which come from Siberia are very dark colored, and are made into cloaks and other warm garments for winter. Gray Squirrels sometimes get together in great numbers, and travel across the country, over mountains and through dense woods, and even swim broad rivers. The little Flying

The Flying Squirrel.

Squirrel is one of the most curious, gentle, and beautiful of living things; it is not often seen, for it is quiet in the daytime, coming out at night for its food. It is a very social little animal, and large numbers often live together in hollow trees. The Chipmunk, or Striped Squirrel, is a very pretty and lively little creature, which makes its nest in a hole which it digs in the ground, near the roots of an old tree, or under the shelter of a wall; the nest is made soft and

warm with dry leaves, and near it is stored a
large supply of walnuts, chestnuts, beechnuts,

The Striped Squirrel, or Chipmunk.

acorns, and grain. In autumn it is very busy
getting its winter store of food, and it is often
seen hurrying along to its hole, with its cheek-
pouches full of nuts or grain.

The Leopard Spermophile, or
Striped Gopher.

The little Leopard Spermophile, or Striped
Gopher, is even prettier than the Chipmunk, its

fur is so beautifully spotted and striped. It lives on the prairies, and digs deep, winding burrows in the ground; sometimes it is seen sitting just at the opening, but if any one comes near it darts, with a chirp, into its hole.

The curious animal called the Prairie Dog also lives on the prairies of the West; it is a short, clumsy-looking little creature, and does not look at all like a dog; but it makes a sharp noise which

The Prairie Dog.

sounds very much like barking, and from this it gets its name. It digs a burrow in the ground, and, at the opening, it raises a little mound of earth. Sometimes hundreds of these little animals make their burrows so near each other that the ground is covered with these mounds, and they look so much like little villages, that the hunters call them " Dog-towns." There is a small kind of owl which is often found living in these burrows with the Prairie Dogs, and sometimes the rattlesnake takes up his abode there, perhaps to feed upon the young of the Prairie Dog.

On the next page there is a picture of the Beaver, with its strong sharp teeth, its webbed hind feet, and its broad, flat tail. Beavers live in and near the water, and they eat the roots of water-plants, and the bark of the birch, willow, maple, and of some other trees; and when they cannot get bark enough they eat the hard wood itself. In order to get the bark to eat, and materials with which to build dams and houses, they gnaw through, and thus cut down with their sharp teeth, trees both small and large, sometimes those that are a foot and a half or two feet in diameter. When they have cut down a tree, they cut off all the limbs, and cut them into pieces one or two feet long or more, and they cut the stem or trunk of the tree into short logs.

Beavers like ponds in which they may swim, and in or near which they can build their houses or lodges, and in whose banks they can dig their burrows; for they have both burrows and houses. Therefore they make dams across the brooks and

The Beaver.

streams of the regions in which they live, so as to form such ponds as they like. They make their dams of poles, and limbs of trees, and brush, mixed with stones and mud. They save all of the bark of the limbs, and of the trunks of the young trees, for food; so that nearly all of the sticks in a beaver-dam are peeled. The dams are very strong, and a man can easily walk from one

side of the river to the other on one of them.
Beavers build their houses or lodges of sticks,
stones, and mud; they are quite large, and the
walls are very thick. The houses stand in the
water, but the nest or room where the Beavers
live is above the surface of the water, and is dry
and warm. From four to eight Beavers, and sometimes as many as twelve, live in one house or
lodge. The only entrance to their houses is
through a hole below the surface of the water,
and the entrance is very neatly made. Near
their houses they sink in the water a large supply
of wood and bark for their food during the winter.
They do most of their work at night; but they
begin very early in the evening, and they also
work early in the morning.

Long ago there were many Beavers in our country, and their old dams and ponds are still found
in many places. But their fur is so fine, and so
beautiful, and makes such warm caps and collars,
and brings so much money to the hunters and
trappers, that they have shot and trapped the
Beavers, till now they are never seen except in
the wild and unsettled regions; and by and by

I fear that they will all be gone. There are many Beavers now living in the swamps and woods near Lake Superior, and if you could go there you would see their dams, and ponds, and houses, and the trees which they have cut down and peeled with their sharp teeth; and you would see the many long canals which the Beavers dig to float their logs in, when the trees which they cut down for their dams, and their food, are far from the pond. Some of their canals are five hundred feet long; they are about three feet wide and two or three feet deep, and partly filled with water. You may perhaps wonder that the Beaver knows so well how to build strong dams, and houses, and to dig canals, and that he knows when and where to store up bark and wood for his winter food. God has made this wonderful animal so that he knows what to do; and He has made all animals so that every one is fitted for the life it is to lead, and the work it has to do.

Young Beavers are sometimes tamed and kept for pets. One was once carried from this country across the Atlantic Ocean, and given to a gentleman in England. He named it "Binny"; and when he called it by its name, it would answer with a little cry, and come to him. It liked to lie upon the hearth-rug, but always wanted to be near its master. Binny liked to eat bread, milk, and sugar ; and he was also fond of roots and tender plants. He wanted to build dams and houses, and so he would get the brooms and sweeping-brushes, and baskets, and books, boots and shoes, clothes, and everything he could find, and try to build them into a dam and a house, just as he would make a dam and a house of poles, sticks, leaves, and mud, if he were in the swamps and woods where he was born.

The Pouched Rat lives in Canada and on the Western prairies, and it makes its nest in

The Pouched Rat, or Pocket Gopher.

little hills or mounds of earth which it throws up. The nest is warmly lined with soft, dry grasses, and with fur which the mother pulls from her own body. Like the mole, it digs burrows very rapidly, and in every direction. It eats roots, and it uses its large pouches to carry food to its nest, and to bring dirt out of its burrow. It is often called the Pocket Gopher.

You have seen the large Rats that live in stables and sometimes in houses. One kind has brown fur, and is called the Brown, or Wharf Rat; another kind has black fur, and is called the Black Rat. They are very hungry fellows, and eat grain, meat, and almost everything they can find; and when they cannot get enough of other food, they kill and eat one another. These two kinds of Rats cannot live together; the Brown Rats are the largest, and they drive off the Black ones, or

The White-footed Mouse.

kill and eat them. There are very many kinds of Rats and Mice, and they are not all so cruel as these large ones. Some of them, like the

House Mouse, the White-footed Mouse, and the little Jumping Mouse, and many others, are very pretty creatures. The Jumping Mouse lives in grain-fields, and leaps over the ground faster than

The Jumping Mouse.

you can run. The largest Rat is the Muskrat. It is smaller than a cat, and has a short, thick body and short legs. It lives in ponds, rivers, and brooks, where it builds a house of mud, sticks, grass, and weeds. Its fur is long and dark, and is often called River Sable.

The Porcupine lives in hollow trees, or in holes among the rocks, and sleeps in the daytime, coming out at night to get its food. It eats bark, leaves, and buds, and is fond of sweet apples and green corn. On the back and tail of the Porcupine grow sharp strong quills. If a dog or any other animal attack it, the quills get into the

The Porcupine.

mouth and cause great pain.   The quills of a
Porcupine which lives in Europe are so long that
they are used for penholders, and are very beautiful.   The Porcupine is larger than a cat, but its
body is rather short.

You have often seen the tame Rabbits hopping
briskly about, or feeding upon the tender grass
and clover buds which they like so well, and you
never tire of watching them; so I think you will
like to read about the little animals which look

so much like Rabbits, and which live in all our
woods and groves; these are the Hares. Many
persons call them Rabbits, but I believe there
are no true Rabbits in the woods of our country.
All the Rabbits which we see are the tame ones,
and these have been brought from Europe. I will
tell you some of the ways in which the Rabbits
differ from the Hares. The Rabbits dig burrows
in the ground, in which they spend much of the
time; the Hares do not dig burrows in which to
live; the Rabbits live together in large numbers;
the Hares live singly, each one by itself. When
the young Rabbit is born, it has a smooth skin,
and its little eyes are shut; but the little Hare
is covered with fur when it is born, and its eyes
are open. When you go to the woods in summer,
you are almost sure to see some of these little
animals; and if you go in the winter, when the
snow is on the ground, you will see the tracks
made by their little feet, and you may see the
Hares themselves, for these active little creatures
do not seek out a snug place when the cold weather
comes, and then go to sleep, and sleep all winter,
as some animals do; but they run about at all

seasons of the year, unless the weather is very,
very cold or stormy, and then they sometimes
shelter themselves in hollow logs or trees, or in
holes in the ground, which some other animal
has made. The Hares are very pretty animals.
Their eyes are large and bright, and are so placed
that the little animal can see nearly all around
itself; their ears are very large, and can be raised
and turned in any direction, and they seem to
catch the faintest sounds. Their fore legs are
short and rather weak, but their hind legs are
long and stout, and the Hares move over the ground
mainly by taking long leaps ; when not frightened,
or when eating, they hop or jump along only a
little way at a time. The Hares eat grass and
tender plants, and the buds and twigs and bark
of shrubs and trees, and they feed at night, or
at twilight, and in the daytime stay upon their
" forms " or nests. The " form " of the Hare is
only a little hollow on the ground ; sometimes the
" form " is near an old log, or in a heap of brush,
or at the foot of a tree, or under a fallen tree-
top ; sometimes it is hidden by the tall grass and
weeds. The Hares have well-trodden paths in

the woods, which lead from one point to another,
and they use these paths both in the summer
and winter. The Hares have a curious habit of
stamping upon the ground with their hind feet
when they are alarmed or excited. They are very
timid creatures, and when frightened they bound
and leap swiftly away, stopping every few moments
to listen to any strange sound. If you see one
of these animals bounding away from you, and if
you whistle to it, it will at once stop and listen,
and if you keep on whistling, and at the same time
walk towards the Hare, you can often get quite
near it. Although the Hare is so timid, it will
sometimes fight bravely for its young. A gentleman once saw a Hare attack a large black snake
which was holding in its coils one of her little
ones. She would spring over the snake, and
strike back upon the snake with her hind feet.
Hares are often hunted with dogs, and they sometimes show almost as much cunning as a fox in
their efforts to get away from the dogs. At first
they leap swiftly away, then turn aside and stop,
and as soon as the dogs have passed them, they
run back on the same track and try to get to

their " form " again.   Sometimes they leap upon a
log and sit motionless, while the dogs sniff around
in plain sight, and quite near them.   Sometimes
they run into a hole in the ground, or into a hollow
tree if there is an opening near the ground.   When
seized, they sometimes utter a sharp, clear cry.
There are more than twenty kinds of Hares in
the forests of our country.   Some kinds have gray
fur; some are of a reddish-brown color; and in
some kinds the color of the fur changes from reddish in the summer to white in winter.   There
is a picture of a Hare with the dogs on the
thirty-ninth page.

THE ANIMALS WITHOUT FRONT TEETH.

ALL the animals of which you have been read-
ing are clothed either with hair, fur, or wool, or

The Armadillo.

they have a smooth skin; but here is one, called
the Armadillo, which has a hard horny shell made
up of many pieces. This animal lives in the warm-
est parts of our country, and digs burrows in the
ground, in which it stays during the daytime.
It eats insects, worms, fruits, and the juicy roots
of plants. Although it looks so clumsy, it can
run faster than a man.

THE POUCHED ANIMALS.

THE little Opossum lives in the Middle, Southern, and Western States. It is about as large as

The Opossum.

a cat, and its home is in the hollows of trees. It sleeps during the daytime, but spends the night in running about for its food; it eats insects, eggs, and birds, and sometimes comes to the hencoop and kills and eats hens and chickens. On the under part of the body is a pouch, in which the mother places her little ones, and there they stay until they can run about. The Opossum is often hunted for its flesh; and sometimes, when wounded a little, it lies quite still and pretends to be dead; but when the hunter is not watching, it jumps up and runs away.

The Kangaroo.

The Kangaroo is a strange animal which lives

in Australia; it does not often walk or run, but takes great leaps with its long hind feet, and when it stops, rests upon its hind feet and its large strong tail. Like the Opossum, the Kangaroo has a pouch on the under part of the body, in which the young ones are carried; and even after they are large enough to run about, if danger is near, they will get into the mother's pouch, and remain till the danger is past.

The Wombat.

The Wombat is another curious animal which also lives in Australia; it feeds upon grass, and burrows in the ground.

THE DUCK-BILLS.

BUT the most curious animal in Australia is the Duck-bill. It lives in the ponds and streams, and digs burrows in the banks. Its fore feet are

webbed, and it is a good swimmer. Its body is
covered with thick short fur, and it has a bill very

The Duck-bill.

much like that of a duck.   Its food is worms and
insects and other small animals.

And now, dear children, if you like to look at
these pictures, and to read these stories, in another little book I will show you pictures and
tell you stories of the beautiful Birds which God
has made to live in the woods, groves, and fields,
and which delight us so much with their pretty
forms, their bright colors, and their sweet songs.

THE END.

www.ingramcontent.com/pod-product-compliance
Lightning Source LLC
Chambersburg PA
CBHW020235030726
47497CB00009B/3106